Foolish Mortals

Foolish Mortals

Jennifer Johnston

headline
review

First published in 2007
by HEADLINE REVIEW
An imprint of HEADLINE PUBLISHING GROUP

3

Cataloguing in Publication Data is available from the British Library

ISBN 978 0 7553 3052 2

Typeset in Centaur MT by Avon DataSet Ltd, Bidford-on-Avon, Warwickshire

Printed and bound in Great Britain by Clays Ltd, St Ives plc

HEADLINE PUBLISHING GROUP
A division of Hachette Livre UK Ltd
338 Euston Road
London NW1 3BH

www.headline.co.uk
www.hodderheadline.com

To H. E. Geoffrey, with much love and many thanks for the kindnesses he has shown me. And, of course, to Jane, and I must not forget Norah, Cat of cats.

Autumn

'He's coming out ...'

My head was filled with coloured reverberations but I heard the words.

Purple, green, yellow.

It was a deep unknown voice.

'Out.'

Red.

Red, flashing in front of my eyes.

Someone had sewn them shut.

I tried to pull them open, to see who had spoken, to see the world.

No luck.

The colours in my head flashed, red and deepest purple, the purple of kings and queens and cardinals.

I laughed inside myself and the pain came.

Wave after wave, filling my body and my head. Nothing, no part of me was free from that pain. The colours deepened into black and I fell.

I seemed to be forever falling.

Beside me someone sighed. Someone was holding my wrist. Was it the same person, I wondered.

I wondered, and then I realised that I was wondering.

Oh dear God.

I heard the words echo in my head.

Oh dear God.

I felt my jaw, my mouth forming the words, opening and closing.

The fingers holding my wrist loosened, fell away.

'What was that he said?'

'Unh?'

'He spoke. He spoke.'

'Sssh.'

'He must be—'

'Sssssh.'

Silence.

I wondered again.

Someone covered my hand with a soft cloth.

They whispered. I could only hear the soft hissing of their breaths as the words pushed out of their mouths.

Clink and then the sound for a moment of running water.

I surprised myself by knowing what these sounds were.

I knew whispers. I knew water. I knew that someone had put a soft cloth over my hand. A chair leg squeaked on the floor and then someone sighed once more.

I knew those words.

Chair.

Cloth.

Water.

My mouth needed water.

I tried to raise my hand, the one that someone had covered with a soft cloth.

Then the pain began again.

Not this time like the coloured pain. No.

Grey.

I could bear this.

I could wonder where I was, who were the whisperers.

I could try to open my eyes.

Oh dear God.

'He spoke again. Henry.'

'Ssssh. Leave him. He's not yet ready.'

Oh dear God.

'Please let me, please. Henry.'

The chair leg scraped again and someone stood beside me. I felt the shadow of someone there on my right-hand side.

Oh dear God.

'Henry.'

'I'm tired.' It was my voice. I spoke quite clearly. I surprised myself by the clarity of my voice.

'Henry. You're going to be all right. Can you hear me? Henry?'

More words.

Shadow.

Henry.

Tired.

Water.

I turned my head away from the voice. I was truly tired. More tired than I could remember ever being. I was weighted down with tiredness. Long and thin, I was, and covered with heavy stones: shoulders, chest, arms, legs, smooth, heavy stones.

Murmurs reached my ears, but meant nothing. Soft steps moved. I went into blackness.

✳   ✳   ✳

Stephanie, who had been his wife, left the room, followed by Dr Cairns, hot on her heels. He closed the door carefully behind him and turned and lookd at her. She was pale, with deep black rings under her eyes.

'Is he . . . ? Will he . . . ?'

The doctor sighed.

'Mrs . . . ummm . . .'

'O'Connor.'

'Yes.' He said the word angrily. He knew. He bloody knew what her name was, but he had a lot of things in his head. Everyone expected you to be sharp. All the time. 'I'm sorry, Mrs O'Connor, of course I . . . Yes. He'll be all right. Broken leg, ribs, collarbone, they'll all mend. Bones mend. I mean to say when he's about sixty or so, arthritis will probably set in. But.' He laughed a little awkwardly. 'That happens to a lot of people, doesn't it?'

'I suppose.'

She chewed at her lip for a moment.

Her teeth were white and very straight.

Expensive, he thought.

'It was really . . . well, I meant in his head. Yes. What do you . . . ummm?'

He pulled himself together.

'Tomorrow morning, Mrs ... O'Connor. We'll know more tomorrow morning. I will be in my consulting rooms at eleven.' Cautiously he put a hand on her arm. 'In the meantime get some rest. Please, do that.'

He turned and walked away down the highly polished corridor. His shoes squeaked as he walked; that embarrassed him slightly.

Stephanie watched him go.

Damn you.

She turned back towards the door of Henry's room and wondered whether to go in again or go home to bed.

Damn you too.

She decided to go home. She'd see about bed when she got there.

Damn everyone, she thought as she ran down the steps from the hospital to the car park. Most especially Henry.

She sat in her car for a few minutes staring out of the window, looking at people coming and going; people with flowers or plastic bags full of clean clothes, bottles of lemon squash, books. One woman carried a large fluffy toy dog with long ears and another a small radio. They walked with purpose.

I'll bring him some flowers tomorrow, she thought, and the children must come in then, both of them. Not of course at the same time, that might be too much for him. That might make him lapse back into unconsciousness again.

She turned the key and set off for home.

* * *

Ciara was at home, sprawled on a pile of cushions on the floor watching *EastEnders*.

'What's for dinner?' she shouted as her mother closed the front door.

Stephanie didn't answer. She hung her coat up and went into the sitting room.

Her daughter waved a hand at her.

'The BBC's really gone mad.'

Two people were kissing on the large screen.

'They're brother and sister. Incest. I mean to say ... What is the world coming to?'

Stephanie picked up the zapper and switched off the set.

'Hey!'

'Your father is still unconscious.'

'Should we care?'

'Darling, don't be like that. Of course we care.'

Ciara got to her feet and stood for a moment or two staring at her mother.

'Sorry,' she said. 'Of course I care. I think he's a bastard but I love him. Is he going to be OK? What do they say?'

'Bones mend. That's what the doctor said.'

'That was all?'

'More or less. I'm seeing him tomorrow morning. I expect he'll have more to say then. We can have omelettes or we can go down the road. Which would you prefer?'

'You look exhausted. Whackerony. I'll do us omelettes. You go to bed.'

'I'll have a bath. I don't know about bed. I'm tired but I don't think I'll be able to sleep. My head's a whirl. Have you not got work to do?'

'Nope. Done it all.' The lying words flew out of her mouth and round the room, like autumn leaves fluttering in the wind.

Stephanie smiled.

They went their ways; Ciara to rattle and bang in the kitchen and think thoughts about her father; Stephanie to the bath where she fell asleep and was wakened by Ciara's voice calling her.

* * *

It was night-time when my eyes opened. The lights in the room were dim. A figure stood by the window. It was a woman. She was watching me.

Ah.

'Who are you?'

I suppose it was less of a cliché than where am I?

She smiled.

'I've come to say goodbye.' Her voice was low, almost like a man's.

'You have to say hello first.'

She moved silently towards me; there was not even the rustle of her skirt nor the slur of a shoe on the polished floor. She put out a hand and touched my face. A breath of a touch, no more.

'Hello.'

My head hurt with the effort to remember.

'Have we met?'

'Oh yes, my dear.'

'I . . . I'm sorry . . .'

7

'You have forgotten me?'

'I . . .'

I didn't know what to say.

She leant over me, her face hovering above mine. I had never seen her before. I could swear that.

She sighed.

'Such inconstancy.'

I closed my eyes.

*   *   *

Stephanie brought flowers the next morning, an extravagant bunch of freesias, deep red, orange, purple and white, whose strong sweet smell she hoped would drown the hospital smell of floor polish and disinfectant. She also brought the *Irish Times* and a Venetian thriller by Donna Leon, in case he might be well enough to feel like light reading.

He was propped against a hill of white pillows, strapped and bandaged; the bruises on his face showed black and purple on his yellow skin. His eyes were closed, but he opened them when he heard the door.

'Hello,' she said.

She stood by the door for a moment, waiting . . . for what, she wondered. Then with an idiotic gesture she waved the bunch of flowers at him. He closed his eyes again.

'Steph?'

'Yes.'

She went across the room and put the flowers down on a table near the window.

'I'll get a nurse to—'

'It is you, isn't it? Steph?'

'Yes. It is. Yes. I am Stephanie.'

'Thank you,' he said.

His voice, she thought, was scratched and faded, like an old shellac record.

She went over to the bed; her crêpe de Chine scarf had been neatly folded and placed on the locker beside him. She picked it up and put the paper and the book in its place. The scarf she unfolded and draped across her shoulders; it was a wonderful red with the faintest of grey-blue traceries across it. She had bought it in Venice many years before when they had been happy. She always had the remembrance of that happiness when she wore it.

'There's nothing to thank me for,' she said and touched his hand, the hand she had covered with the scarf the night before. 'I've brought you the *Irish Times*. I didn't know if . . .'

'That is good,' he said.

His hand twitched under hers. He scrabbled at her fingers, tried to clasp them, but she pulled away.

'The children will be coming in . . .'

'No,' he said.

He opened his eyes as wide as he could and stared up at her. He flipped his hand at her.

'Not yet. Please.'

'They want to see you. It's been over a year since—'

'No.'

'All right. I'll tell them not to come.'

'I want to be able to think when I see them. I want to be able to remember their names.'

His eyes drooped shut.

She looked at him for a while and then turned and left the room.

At the door she stopped for a moment.

'Donough and Ciara,' she said.

At eleven o'clock precisely she knocked on the door of Dr Cairns's room.

'Come in.'

His secretary looked up from some papers.

'Mrs O'Connor?'

'That's right.'

'Doctor is expecting you. Go right in.'

She nodded towards a door on her left.

The doctor got up when she came into the room. He held out a hand.

'Mrs O'Connor. Good morning. Was I grumpy yesterday? Don't tell me. I know I was. Please sit down. I'd had a dreadful day. The bedside manner wears thin from time to time. I hope you will forgive me.'

She sat down.

'Not at all. I mean, yes, of course. I . . . I saw him earlier. I just popped in. I brought him some flowers. I thought he seemed better. He knew me. That was better. Wasn't it?'

'Yes.' He picked up a pen and tapped the table with it.

Rat-a-tata-tat. Quite rhythmic and soft.

'Am I right in thinking that you and Mr O'Connor are separated?'

'Divorced, actually.'

Ratatata ratatatat.

'I don't really see what—'

'How long?'

'Several years. Look ...'

'How long, to be exact?'

'Two years. It seems like forever.'

'Mrs O'Connor, it seems to me that you are taking on your shoulders the role of next of kin. Do you really think this is what my patient would want?'

'It doesn't really matter, does it? Someone has to care.'

'He has a wife? Hasn't he? Didn't he marry again?'

'She was killed in the accident. Did no one tell you that? Dear God, do you think he doesn't know?'

The rattatting faltered.

'That is likely. Yes. He has been unconscious until last night. I don't know what, if anything, he remembers, about the accident, about anything at all. As I said to you yesterday, his bones will mend, but no one can say anything about his head. Not yet. It will take time. He may be perfectly all right, but ...'

He looked at the pen and then dropped it onto the table. He sighed.

'I'm sorry,' he said at last. 'I can't say much more to you until ... well, until I discover more about who ... You have children?'

'Two.'

'Yes. Grown up?'

'Well ...'

'Perhaps if one of them or both of them were to come and see me.'

Stephanie got to her feet.

'I'll talk to them, but if I may say so, Doctor, I think you are a bloody pain in the ass.'

He looked startled.

'Mrs . . . ah . . .'

'O'Connor.'

'Yes. Yes. I do remember your name. You must realise that your . . . ah, that Mr O'Connor is very ill. I have to be aware of his best interests. You seem to me to be a rather intemperate lady.'

'Possibly. But I am the person who cares. I've told you that.'

He waved a hand in her direction.

'I was his wife for over twenty years. I am the mother of his children. I do care, Doctor. Believe me. Goodbye.'

She stamped out of the room and past his secretary and out of the door into the passage. She left both doors open behind her; why bother slamming them, she thought, as she stamped down the passage.

She stood at the top of the steps outside the hospital main door and looked across the car park. She took a deep breath of fresh air.

'I care,' she shouted. No one paid any attention.

*   *   *

A nurse came into my room and asked me what I would like for lunch.

I told her I wasn't hungry.

She said I must try something.

'Soup, perhaps. A few spoonfuls of soup?'

I didn't answer her.

'You must eat something.'

I shut my eyes.

I could feel the pain starting again. A distant wave which I knew would grow and grow, wash over me, wave upon wave like the tide creeping in, like the sparkling heads tossing, like the undertow pulling gently at first and then washing, pulling, sucking, tugging on and on. I groaned.

Featherlike fingers touched my forehead, slid down over my cheekbone, my jaw, to my neck. I forced my eyes open to see her face; it was the same face, pale as death. I had never seen her before and yet . . .

Her fingers touched my forehead again. She whispered warm words into my ear. I couldn't make out what she was saying, but her breath was warm.

The wave of pain washed, washed washed.

✳ ✳ ✳

'Well one of you will have to go and see the doctor. He won't talk to me. He thinks I'm up to no good and then of course I was rude to him.'

'Trust you. The words fall out of your mouth before you think. Don't they?'

'And Daddy. Just pop in and say hi. He is after all your father.'

Donough sighed.

'Yes, yes, yes, yes.'

'Say your name. Tell him your name, just in case . . .'

'In case of what?'

'Just in case. He might be a bit dopey. You know. He said . . .'

She stopped. She turned away from her son and looked out of the window. Someone had left a deckchair in the middle of the lawn and its seat flapped, dispirited, in the wind. Brown leaves lifted and then fell again, the trees were nearly bare and in the low sun the shadows of their bare branches danced on the grass.

'He said what?' her son asked.

'Nothing much. Just that he mightn't recognise you: any of you. He didn't want that to happen . . . so he said . . .'

'Yes?'

'Not to come.'

'Well there you are then.'

'But . . .'

Donough sighed again.

'I think you should. I really do; and go and see the doctor. Get some sense out of him.'

'No. I won't go.'

'You said yes a few minutes ago.'

'You hadn't told me the whole of it. About him saying that.'

'For heaven's sake Donough, stop arguing. I want you to go and see the man.'

'You're bullying me.'

She began to cry. She felt in her pocket for a tissue and dabbed at her face. He watched her in silence for a few moments and then got up and went over to her. He put his arms around her.

'It's OK, Ma. I'll go. Tomorrow morning, I'll go. Come on, don't cry. Please don't cry. Everything's going to be all right.' He rocked her in his arms and kissed the top of her head. 'Mamma mia, sssh. Don't cry. There, there, there.'

She lifted her head and gazed out at the garden over his shoulder.

'Someone's left a deckchair out there.'

'I'll get it.'

She dabbed at her eyes again.

'Thank you.'

He unlocked the door and went out into the garden. She watched him pick up the deckchair, fold its legs together and carry it over to the shed on the other side of the lawn; the leaves scuttered round his legs as he walked and she thought of Henry, his whole unbroken self, cutting down the apple trees and putting up the shed and how angry she had been with him. They had been lovely apple trees, Beauty of Bath, pink, crunchy and sweet. She could taste the juice in her mouth as she thought about it. You couldn't buy Beauty of Bath in the shops any longer, she couldn't think why. Maybe you never could buy them. Maybe only those people privileged enough to have apple trees in their gardens had ever tasted Beauty of Bath apples. Henry had not cared; he had preferred the shed, so that his expensive garden tools might not get wet, where he could keep things in order. He had used the work bench quite a lot. She wondered how he managed without it now, in his new life, and then thought that now his new life was changed, he had entered a new phase.

'He needn't think he's going to come back here.'

'What?' asked Donough as he closed the door behind him.

'I was just thinking about your father. I didn't realise I'd spoken. I didn't mean to speak aloud.'

'You're a terror for uncontrolled speaking.'

'Life goes in fits and starts, but forwards, always forwards. I don't want to go back to all that.'

'I don't suppose he will either.'

'You're probably right.'

'While we're talking ...' He paused and licked his lips. 'I've got a house. Em. Yes. Mespil Road, looking out on the canal.' He laughed nervously. 'Jolly nice.'

Stephanie looked at him for a while, trying to collect her thoughts, trying not to allow herself to fall into uncontrolled speech. She smiled finally.

'Great, darling. That's wonderful. I didn't know you were looking.'

'On and off. This just came up and it sounded too good to miss.'

'Terribly expensive?'

'Could be worse. You must come and see it. The painters are there at the moment and we've put in another bathroom. Nowadays you have to have two bathrooms.'

'Of course. You say we. Who do you ...?'

'Brendan.'

'Oh.'

He put his hand on her shoulder.

'It was going to happen sometime or other, Ma. You know that. We're not kids any longer. Time to move out. Lead lives of quiet desperation like everyone else. You like Brendan. You know you do.'

'Yes, I do. I just thought ... well are you sure? Really sure?'

'Yes, darling, I'm sure. And he's sure too. We've talked a lot about this. We're doing the right thing. Don't worry about us. It's going to be fine.'

They stood there; he held her shoulder for a long time without speaking, then she looked up into his face and kissed his cheek.

'That's OK by me, son. I just want my kids to be happy and then I think, what's happy but a terrible illusion? And we keep pushing them towards this thing that barely exists. Pushing gently but nonetheless pushing. We always think we have an overview, that we are right, but we seldom are. I think it's time for a drink, don't you? I'll have a large gin and tonic.'

He laughed. He took his hand from her shoulder. He touched her hair.

'Thanks Ma. You're a star.'

* * *

Bright autumn morning fell in squares on the floor.

I was washed and ready for the day, whatever that might bring: doctors, nurses, assessments, reassessments, pokers and pryers.

All I wanted was to remember what had happened.

It's all right, they say, it will all come back in time.

All I had in my head was the grinding sound of metal, and the engine's squeal as if it were being pushed beyond endurance and then a voice crying Nooooo, which was probably my voice pitched so hectically that even my own mother wouldn't have recognised it.

I was wearing blue-and-white striped pyjamas, which I didn't very much like, and there was a thin gold ring on the third finger of my left hand. That was clear, unequivocal. I was a married man.

And Stephanie had come to visit me and talked about children. Yes. And she had brought me flowers which sat there on the windowsill in a blue bowl, in the sunlight.

I could hear feet on the corridor and an occasional laugh.

If I keep very still I have no pain.

The woman who visits me in the darkness who whispers warm words into my ear is not Stephanie. Today I am determined to find out the wheres and whos and whys of my current situation.

Donough.

I remember. That is a name I remember.

Suddenly I see her face, pale, drained of energy but so happy.

'Pick him up,' she had said. 'He is yours too.'

And I had bent and picked up the tiny creature from the cradle and held him in my hands. That was where he fitted, in my two hands.

She had laughed and a little colour flushed into her face.

'You look so frightened. Don't be frightened. He won't break.'

'His head might fall off.'

She laughed again and I had felt so happy, that she had laughed, that this creature there in my hands was mine. I held him up to my face and kissed his cheek. She patted the bed and I sat beside her and we both stared at our child, in my hands, and smiled and were at that moment happier than anyone in the world had ever been before.

Damn, I thought to myself. Damn, damn, damn.

I drifted off and then the doctor came. I opened my eyes and saw him standing over me, my wrist held delicately between his fingers.

'Doctor?'

'Yes.'

He placed my hand gently on the bedcover and wrote something in his notebook.

'Yes, yes.'

'Well first of all, where am I?'

'Vincent's.'

'And why?'

'I would have thought that was . . . hum . . . yes . . . well as the result of a motor accident. You have multiple injuries, but nothing life-threatening. Ribs, collarbone and leg. You'll be as good as new in a few weeks. Anything else?'

'Where did it happen? How . . .'

'How I can't tell you, but it seems you ran slap bang wallop into the wall of Blackrock College, just down the road. A mile, half a mile. Car was a total write-off.'

He smiled happily at me.

'You mean I ran into—'

'No, no, no. Not you, the driver.'

'Who was the driver?'

He stopped smiling.

'I was rather hoping that we might have a few more days' recovery time before . . .'

'Doctor.'

'Well actually . . .' He bent and picked up my hand again. 'We think it was your wife.' He squeezed my fingers.

'My wife?'

'Yes. I'm terribly sorry. She, ah, was killed instantly. No pain, nothing like that at all. Her brother came and identified her.'

He replaced my hand on the bed and stood looking at me.

'My wife?'

That did puzzle me.

'Stephanie. Surely she—'

'Charlotte. Your wife's name was Charlotte.'

It was as if the corner of a curtain in my mind was tweaked and something moved behind it. I closed my eyes for a moment or perhaps it was more than a moment because when I opened them the doctor was gone.

'Charlotte.' I spoke the word aloud.

I heard the shadow of a laugh.

Later that morning Donough came in. Awkwardly he carried a bunch of flowers, dahlias, picked from the remaining ones in the garden; now how did I remember that, I wondered.

'Donough,' he said as he laid the flowers on the table by the bed. 'Your son.'

'I know.'

I held out my good hand towards him and tentatively he touched it.

'You remember me?'

'Why wouldn't I?'

He shrugged. Then he gave me quite a pleasant little smile.

'It's been a long time. Nearly two years. The last time we met was the night of my graduation. Do you remember? Probably not. We were all poleaxed. In the Lincoln ... even Mum was there and you came in and ...' His eyes filled suddenly with tears. 'I'm sorry,' he said. 'Really, really sorry.'

'I don't remember, son, I have to admit I haven't got control of my remembering yet.'

'You brought a bottle of champagne and . . . and you handed it to me and said, "Congratulations, son." And I said we don't want your bloody champagne, so fuck off.'

He put his head in his hands and began to cry.

'Hey,' I said. 'Hey. Don't cry, son. Please don't – there must have been a good reason for such intemperance.'

'Oh yes. Yes, of course there was, but . . . but I would like to say here and now that not a day has passed since then without me wishing that I had never said it. So here we are now and you don't remember and I am apologising. Sorry, Dad.'

'Em, thanks. That's OK, son. Let's leave it at that, shall we?'

We were silent for a while.

'So,' I said eventually. 'What are you doing now? With your life? What sort of job do you have?'

'I'm a sub-editor on the *Irish Times*. Working nights. Hoping that one day soon I'll get a foot on the ladder. Up, up the ladder.'

'I'm sure you will. That sounds good. Did I know about this?'

'I think you knew about everything. I don't believe you stopped caring.'

'I'm sure I didn't.'

'Mum wants to know if you need washing done, anything like that, you know, shopping. Anything.'

'Tomorrow. I'll know more tomorrow.'

'Ciara will be in tomorrow.'

'Ciara?'

I saw a flash of long red hair. I heard intemperate laughter, just for a moment.

'Hair. Long red hair.'

He nodded.

'She's still at school. She's up to her eyes at the moment. She does her leaving next summer. She's nice. You'll like her. She has the most amazing hair. I'm not surprised you remember that.'

He stood up.

'I must go. I'm glad ... you'll be OK. I'm glad ... I'll be in again.' He touched my hand again. 'Take care.' He went red in the face. 'God, what a stupid thing to say.'

'I will try not to fall out of bed.'

'Yes. Bye, Dad. See you.'

He waved his hand at me and left.

Things could not be too bad. I could remember the colour of my younger daughter's hair.

I must begin to bend my mind towards Charlotte.

All those whys and wherefores.

For the moment I was tired so I closed my eyes.

In my sleep she came to me again.

Someone came.

She held my hand, her thumb rotated on the back of my wrist and she whispered words to me that I couldn't catch.

'What?' I bent my head towards her. 'What? Sorry but I can't ... I didn't quite get that. Do speak up. Yes. Up.'

She smiled and continued to whisper.

Someone.

The feel of her hand was good and her thumb circling, circling.

* * *

Grey mist was falling from the sky, making everything damp and slimy.

I really don't like autumn, she thought; it's beautiful and colourful, but carries with it, flaunts in fact, the inevitability of winter.

She was alone in the house.

She had always liked that. She liked to breathe the air unbreathed by anyone else. She liked the emptiness, the knowledge that there was no one behind any door, no voice would call her, no footstep disturb the tranquil silence. When she wasn't working she listened to music, the slow mournful coiling and uncoiling of Monteverdi or Pergolesi; Schubert, 'il supremo' she called him in her mind, and of course Johann Sebastian Bach. She worked in silence. Tapped out on her processor tight, bleak short stories about the relationships between men and women.

Now she was reading and thinking intermittently about Henry.

What, she wondered, would happen to him when he came out of hospital?

I can keep an eye on him, but have him here, occupy myself fully . . . heavens no. No. I must take a stand. No. That sounds too dramatic. There must be no dramatics. I will just leave him be in his own flat and keep a weather eye out. Make sure he doesn't dwindle away. Like not eating properly. I'm damned if I'll do his laundry though. Uh-huh. That he can sort out for himself. Supposing though he isn't able? Can't put his dirties into the machine and switch it on. He was never able to do that when he was here. Why should things be different now? Maybe

he learnt lessons from Charlotte. Ha ha. Bitter laughter. He is
not my business any longer. Ay, thank God for that. My mother
always said he was the wrong man for me. Even when we were
happy she said that. And we were happy. I distinctly remember
that.

The sound of the hall door scraping on the tiles;
automatically she thought I must get that seen to, an automatic
thought she'd had for over two years now.

'Yoo-hoo.'

Donough's voice.

'Sitting room.'

He came in and slung his briefcase on the floor.

'Hi. Filthy day.'

'Umm.'

He sat on the sofa and leaning his head on the back of it
stared up at the ceiling. For a moment or two neither of them
spoke.

'I went to see him.'

'That's good. How was he?'

'Not too bad. His memory's shot, but I think he'll be fine.
Time is what he needs. The doctor wasn't there. But the ward
sister was quite cheery about him. I told him Ciara would be in
tomorrow.' He gave a little laugh. 'He remembered her red hair.
I thought that was pretty good.'

'Not bad.'

'Pale and wan.'

'Yes.'

'Only to be expected of course. I . . . ah . . . apologised.'

She was startled.

'Whatever for?'

'My graduation day.'

She thought for a moment.

'Oh that! I had forgotten about that.'

'So had he.'

She laughed.

'I felt better. It's something I've felt rotten about.'

She patted his shoulder.

'Personally I thought it was pretty noble of you. Rude, of course, but noble.'

Donough waved his hands in the air.

'I'm a hero?'

'I wouldn't go quite that far.' She got up. 'I must go and make the dinner.'

'Count me out. I'm on the early shift, and I won't be back tonight.'

She left the room without saying anything.

He hated that. He had done nothing wrong. He was the way he was. It was nothing to do with her. She was not complaining, never, but she wished he were not the way he were, she couldn't help showing it in her face.

She stood in the kitchen, angry with herself for having been upset.

Bloody, bloody, she thought.

Idiot.

Why do I always get this stab of regret?

Why, why do I wish him to be like everyone else?

What a fate!

I don't mind other people's children being like that. But mine?

No.

People say it is the mother's fault. What have I done wrong?

It's the way you were born. That's what he said to me many times.

Many, many times.

It's in the blood, genes, whatever you like to call it, and where's the harm?

I wonder if Henry knows?

He had gone before Donough told me.

One night in the kitchen. The wind was rattling the panes and rain was lashing down and he had blurted it out, just sitting there opposite me at the table, the dirty dishes around us.

'I think I should tell you,' he had said, cool as a cucumber, it seemed to me. 'I prefer boys to girls, men to women. In fact—'

I had held up my hand, like a policeman on point duty.

'Wait,' I had said. 'Just a moment. Are we having a joke? Do you know what you are saying?'

He threw back his head and laughed.

'Sure I know. I'm telling you something that I don't think you had noticed and I'm telling you before someone else does. Ciara might, brat that she is. I am gay, bent, queer, homosexual, call it what you will. I don't care. I just thought you ought to know.'

I was flabbergasted.

After a little while I asked him if he were sure and he laughed again.

'Sure, Ma. As sure as I will ever be about anything.'

He got up and kissed the top of my head. Then he held my hand for a while. I don't remember what happened after that.

I don't mind.

I really don't mind.

I just get this stab of regret from time to time, about which I seem to be able to do nothing.

Bloody, bloody, bloody.

*   *   *

'What day is it?' I asked the nurse as she put a cup of tea on the table that went across my bed.

'Thursday, love,' she answered. 'Don't ask me the date. I never know the date.'

She patted my cheek.

'How long have I been in here? I must begin to orientate myself.'

'Near on a week now. Friday. Yes. It'll be a week tomorrow.'

'It's like looking at the world through a fog. I know there's lots of stuff there, but I can't see it.'

'It'll be all right. You'll see. A few more days and the fog will lift. You got a nasty bang on the head. Have you seen your two lovely black eyes?'

'No.'

She laughed.

'You're in for a treat.'

She unhooked the glass that was above the basin and handed it to me.

Cautiously I peeped.

'Oh my God.'

The top half of my face was an amazing concoction of colours.

'And nothing was broken?'

'Nothing in your head. That's a tough old skull you have there. That tea's hot, don't scald yourself. No need to add to your miseries.'

She bustled out of the room.

Carefully I lifted the teacup to my lips.

Carefully.

My fingers trembled with the weight of the cup.

Carefully I took a sip and carefully placed the cup once more on its saucer.

I must not scald myself, I said inside my head.

The words tickled my memory.

'You have my heart scalded,' Mother used to say to me and I used to laugh. I heard her voice in my head, low melodious notes. Slightly plaintive. 'Henry, you have my heart scalded.'

What had I done to scald the heart of a woman with such a beautiful voice?

I was standing in the drawing room, shifting from foot to foot; she sat at her desk, her hair in a heavy roll at the back of her neck. She looked at her hands clasped and looked in the desk in front of her.

'I am not worried for Stephanie and the children, but for you. I don't think you know what you want. I think you're behaving like an idiot. I love Steph. You know that. She's bright. She can cope, even with a broken heart, it's you. Sometimes you make me despair.' She turned and looked directly at me; her eyes were large and very blue. 'What do you want, Henry?'

'Mother, I'm forty-eight . . .'

'I know. I really do know what age you are . . . to the minute. You're behaving like an adolescent. You are doing something that in three or four years you will regret and you don't know why. Stupidity. That's what I call it. Stupidity.'

For a few moments neither of us spoke. She stared at her hands again.

'Not that I have anything against Charlotte. It's you. You are the messer. You are the mucker. She's a decent woman, but she doesn't know what . . .' She stopped.

'She doesn't know what?' I asked.

'She doesn't know anything. She doesn't know what you want. She doesn't know the way you are . . . the sort of you, not a bloody thing about you. I know.'

'You're being really very tiresome. This is a ridiculous conversation. I am going to marry Charlotte. It's none of your business.'

'Of course it's my business. You're throwing away a life that you've tolerated for twenty years and you could quite well tolerate for another twenty. Throwing away those lovely children and——'

'I am not throwing away my children.'

'Henry, Henry, Henry, you don't know what you're doing. Now go away and leave me in peace. You have my heart scalded.'

It came back to me, bright and clear, like the sound of church bells on a summer Sunday morning.

I must try to understand.

Instead I fell asleep.

And in my sleep she came to me again, that enigmatic woman, and she spoke to me. Her voice was sweet and husky, like treacle, I thought. The words fell from her mouth and flew out through the window, up towards the stars. I couldn't make out what she was saying to me, but I could see the words tumbling in the sky, multicoloured words.

How could I understand?

How?

✳ ✳ ✳

'I really hate funerals.' Stephanie poured milk into her coffee as she spoke.

'Don't go then.'

'I wasn't asking for advice, I was merely stating a fact. Just musing aloud.'

Ciara rolled her eyes and munched her toast.

'Well if I were you . . .'

'You're not. More coffee?'

'No thanks, I must fly.' She got to her feet, toast in hand. 'I would not go. Not, not.' She waved the toast towards her mother, causing marmalade to fall onto the floor.

'Now look what you've done.'

'No probs.'

She shoved the remains of the toast into her mouth, bent and gave the carpet a little rub with her finger, wiped her finger on her trousers, gave her mother's cheek a sticky peck and was gone, all in one movement.

'If you're going enjoy it.' Her voice floated back from the hall and then the door banged.

'Thanks,' muttered Stephanie.

Should I bring flowers? she wondered.

Should I send flowers from Henry?

If so, how flamboyant should they be?

Or just a token?

After all she had tried to kill him.

Hadn't she?

Why would she have done such a thing?

Will he remember when his mind comes to itself again?

Will he know why?

Will he want to know why?

Perhaps one rose. A beautiful white rose, at its peak, the centre fading to pink. She closed her eyes and saw the flower, saw the glossy green leaves and the thorns on the stem, smelt the faint sweet scent. That would be appropriate. No message, just the perfect rose.

I never tried to kill him; such a thought never entered my mind. I was too busy crying, feeling sorry for myself and at the same time trying to show the world how brave and strong I was. And the children; I had to show them that I could live without their father, that we could continue to be a happy family, that none of us would suffer. Lord, what fools these mortals be! Shakespeare, of course, the man who has a word or two for everything. In the end of all I was right. Buckets of tears, but no blood. It's better not to have blood or broken bones. I kept my tears for the darkness and I would lie in bed and muffle my sobbing with my pillow until I fell asleep, and wake the next morning with my eyes red and a basket full of obnoxious Kleenex beside the bed.

I remember so well one morning, quite out of the blue, the doorbell rang and there on the step stood Tash, wrapped in a bright scarlet shawl against the late autumn cold. I hadn't seen her since he had left. She had looked amazingly angry and swept past me into the house. I watched her cross the hall and stride towards the kitchen.

'Coffee,' she shouted back at me as she strode.

'Tash.' I hurried after her, afraid of what she might do in the kitchen. 'I promise you this isn't my fault.'

'I know it's not, you bloody damn fool.' She threw herself into the large wicker chair by the window, where I had been working, and began to pull my papers, pens and books out from under her behind and throw them onto the floor, followed by her shawl. 'I told him he was a fool. I told him he didn't know what he was doing. Coffee please dear, I came out without having any breakfast. Why haven't you been in touch with me? I just felt so angry this morning when I got up. Furious. Raging. I have been expecting you to ring all week.'

'Do you want some toast?' I lit the gas under the kettle. 'I had to get my head around it before I talked to anyone. Mind that stuff, Tash, it's work.'

'No toast. Just strong, black coffee. Killer coffee. Why didn't you ring me? I am, after all . . .'

'I thought . . .'

'His mother. I obviously didn't bring him up very well, did I?'

'I thought you might be thinking that it was all my fault.'

'Did I? Answer my question. Did I or did I not bring him up well?'

'He always seemed OK to me.'

'Blame. We always have to search for someone else to blame. It's bloody awful. We used to know, have certainties, what was right and what was wrong. Now everything is in such a muddle. I did not teach him what was right and what was wrong. Oh my God.'

'Do shut up, Tash. He's forty-eight. He ought to be able to work things out for himself by now. He fell in love. I thought he loved me, but there you are. I thought he loved the kids too much ever to want to do this to them.'

'He doesn't love this woman.'

I spooned a lot of coffee into the coffee pot.

'I know.'

I poured boiling water over the grounds.

'You say nothing.'

'What is there to say?'

'You could agree with me.'

'No, I couldn't do that.'

'I hope you're going to fight, to keep him. Fight hard, fight dirty if need be.'

I shook my head.

'No?' She had screamed the word at me.

'Tash . . .'

'You must not let him make this terrible mistake.'

I pushed down the plunger in the coffee pot with such vigour that coffee splashed out of the lip onto the table.

'Get off my back, for heaven's sake.'

She began to cry, huge tears spouting from her eyes and falling like rain around her and then I began also to cry, only in a more restrained fashion. I stood in the middle of the floor and snuffled and she sat in the chair and bawled. How lucky, I thought at that moment, that there was no one else in the house. After a while we both stopped and began to mop up.

'Nothing like a good cry,' said Tash. 'I'm ready for my coffee now and I think I will have a piece of toast.'

Stephanie laughed at the recollection.

Poor old Tash.

I wonder if she wants to come to the funeral.

No, no, no. Not with me.

Better get my skates on.

I have to get dressed.

I have to get a rose.

I have to polish up my sympathetic smile.

✻   ✻   ✻

Two nurses bustled round the room.

'Sister says we must get you up,' said the one with the blonde hair.

'Well, you can tell Sister that I'm quite happy where I am.'

They giggled.

'You don't have to get dressed, she said, just for now, but up you must get.'

She puffed some pillows and made the chair by my bed look comfortable.

Outside it was raining and the window was spotted with wriggling tadpole drops.

'You'll hurt me getting me out.'

They giggled again.

'Not at all. You'll feel much better when you're up. Everyone does. It's psychological as much as anything else.' She pulled down the bedcover and I lay there feeling foolish dressed in some kind of white smock, one leg in plaster with my grey toes peering at me over the edge.

'My toes are grey,' I said.

The blonde nurse put her arm behind my back carefully and her partner took my legs and they swivelled so that before I knew where I was I was sitting on the edge of the bed with my feet on the ground.

'There you are. That didn't hurt you, did it?'

'I'm not there yet.'

'You can do the rest yourself. Take my arm and stand up on one foot and then turn yourself into the chair. Not too fast, remember your ribs.' I closed my eyes for a moment and then did as she said.

'Now, isn't that great.' She tucked a blanket round me and patted my head in a friendly way.

'What's your name?' I asked her.

'Nurse. They're all called nurse. So that's that.' The voice came from the door; Sister stood there watching with a slight smile on her face. 'Well done. I'm sure he'd like a cup of tea now. Would you not?'

'I would indeed.'

She nodded and the two girls left the room. She remained planted in the doorway. 'You'll be as right as rain in a few weeks. You'll see.' She took a couple of steps towards me. 'Mr O'Connor. There's something I must tell you.'

'What's that?'

'Your wife . . .'

As she said the word I felt my forehead creasing into a frown.

'. . . is being buried today.'

I didn't say anything. I rubbed at my forehead with my hand. She must have taken this as a sign of distress as she came over, right beside me, and put her hand on my arm.

'Charlotte, that's her name isn't it? is being buried today. Her brother telephoned and asked us to let you know.'

'I . . .'

'He said he would deal with flowers and all that. He said to say that she was being buried in Dean's Grange, in her family plot.'

'Oh yes. Thank you, Sister. Yes. Thank you.'

She took her hand from my arm.

'Will you be all right?'

'Yes. Thank you. I'll be ... thank you.'

She left the room.

> *The da-ay thou ga-a-vest Lo-rd is ended,*
> *The darkness falls at thy behest;*
> *To thee our morning hymns ascended.*
> *Thy praise shall sa-anctif-y our rest.*

The organist played at some lugubrious speed of his own invention; the rector closed his eyes as he sang, though whether this was because of extreme sorrow at my father's death or a comment of his own on the organist I couldn't tell. My mother sniffled beside me into her shawl and when I looked towards Stephanie her eyelid moved in the shadow of a wink. I tried not to smile. The church was filled with distinguished members of the Bar, my father's colleagues, and a smile would have been inappropriate. That would have been an age ago ... summer, it was summer. I remember standing outside the church shaking hands with people and the sun beating down on us all. We were still happy then, I remember that well. I remember how she tucked her hand into my elbow and squeezed my arm and I was so happy to know that her smiling face belonged to me. Mother sniffled for about a week and then cheered up and began to paint again.

We were happy then ... Well I suppose happy on and off, like most people, but I can remember the warmth I felt when I looked at her in the church and she winked at me, a warmth that hit me in the pit of my stomach and then gently spread through my whole system.

So be it, Lord; thy thro-one shall never
Like earth's proud empi-ires pass away:
Thy kingdom stands and grows forever,
Till all thy cre-eatures o-own thy sway. A-a-amen.

My brother George and I and four cousins carried the coffin out of the church to the hearse, while the congregation respectfully stood and stared at us and my mother and Stephanie and the children walked slowly behind us; the organist fortissimo and very slowly ground out some solemn Bach piece, and the people shuffling out of the church began to relax their faces in the warmth of the summer sun.

My head began to throb.

I wondered how long it would be before they decided to put me back again in my bed. I was sure my head wouldn't throb when I was safely and comfortably back there.

George. Why had he not been to see me?

Oh, God I felt so seedy and exhausted. My shoulder was hurting and my leg itched inside the plaster and I had that idiotic hymn stuck now in my mind like a cracked record.

The da-ay thou gavest Lord is . . .

Someone would have to bring me some books to read.

. . . the darkness falls at . . .

And George. George. I would like to see George.

✢ ✢ ✢

I shouldn't have come.

Stephanie stopped halfway up the hill to the church; she could hear the organist playing something reflective. The hearse stood outside the door, its back open wide and waiting. Two men sat motionless in the front seats. The rain was relentless. Away to the right, beyond the rooves, you could just see the grey sea. She twiddled the perfect rose in her fingers; she had wrapped the long stem in a red ribbon and wondered whether she should remove it; it had a frivolous look to it that might, she thought, be misunderstood.

A man brushed past her and then stopped and turned.

'Steph!'

She looked up from the rose.

'George. Dear George. How amazing. I thought you were in Toronto.'

'I was until last night. I've just come from the airport. I tried to ring you from the taxi.'

They kissed, then he drew her hand into the crook of his elbow.

'Come, we'll weather this together. I was afraid I might be all alone, or with Mother.'

They crunched up the hill.

'How is Henry?'

'I think he's going to be OK. He's a bit broken up, but it's his memory they're worried about.'

'I will go and see him after this and if I could have a bed with you, I'm going back tomorrow.'

'So soon?'

'I must, darling. I'm a busy businessman and busy business doesn't wait for anything, births, deaths or marriages. What's with the rose?'

'It's from Henry. I thought . . . do you think I should take the ribbon off?'

He shook his head.

They were at the church door. She closed her umbrella and shook it. He took it from her.

'I'll take that and give me the rose, I'll put it on the coffin.' Without a word she handed him the rose and followed him into the church. There were not many people there and she slipped into a pew at the back and sat down. She watched George as he walked up the nave and placed the rose on the coffin. A man stepped from the front pew and spoke to him; George put his hand on the man's shoulder and leant towards him speaking softly in his ear. Stephanie groaned quite loud and the woman in front of her turned and looked at her. She bent her head and covered her face with her hands. She heard George's feet clacking towards her and moved backwards slightly for him to pass her. He touched her shoulder briefly and sat down.

'That was her brother,' he said in a low voice. 'He was defending his right to put flowers on the coffin. He alone. When I said the rose was from Henry, he saw reason. He wanted us both to go and sit up there with him. I said no.'

'Oh God, I'm so glad you are here. I'd never have coped with that.'

'I hate funerals. I don't want one. Will you remember that Steph? Just throw me in the sea, or something like that.'

'I don't think the Department of Health would let us.'

'Well anything, but not this sort of rubbish.'

The organ played a warning chord and everyone stood up. The rector appeared from the vestry, moved quickly to the front of the altar and spread his arms towards the congregation.

'We brought nothing into this world, and it is certain that we can carry nothing out. The Lord gave, and the Lord hath taken away; blessed be the name of the Lord.'

They sat down.

The church was dark, grey light filtered through the tall windows, and there were little pricks of yellow from the wall sconces. Tap and trickle the rain went on the windows and through the running water she could see the branches of the trees tossing their remaining leaves away. George looked grey too, tired from his journey; she felt that if he closed his eyes in prayer it might be hours before he was able to open them again. Sleep would entrap him. Poor, nice George.

He had cried as he carried the coffin at his father's funeral. The undertaker had seen the unrestrained tears and guided him down the two low steps out of the church.

The sun had been shining that day.

George had come back from Canada for that ceremony also, filled with anger at herself and Henry for not having told him that his father was dying.

'Why did no one tell me?' They were the first words he had spoken when they met him at the airport. No hellos or good-to-see-yous. Henry had put his arms around his brother.

'We didn't know, bro. Honest to God. He was the same as usual one day, confused, disorientated, mad, if you like, poor old sod, and they rang us in the middle of the night to say he was dead. No one could have known. I promise you that.'

'I would like to have seen him before he died.'

'No you wouldn't. It was not a happy thing to see him. Everything gone. No bloody spark.'

'But still . . .'

'*But still nothing. When you last saw him he was fine, upstanding. Keep that in your memory.*'

George had nodded but had borne a tiny grudge.

Well she thought, grudges or no grudges, here he was now, more power to him.

He smiled a grey smile in her direction and she reached out and took his hand.

They sat and stood so, hand in hand, while the rector spoke and the brother spoke and the rector prayed:

'Grant, O Lord, to all who are bereaved, the spirit of faith and courage that they may have strength to meet the days to come with steadfastness and patience ...'

'Amen,' said the congregation and their hands loosened and they stood up in solemnity as the men from the undertakers carried the coffin down the aisle. It was followed by the brother, a man of such extreme beauty that Stephanie gasped aloud when he came into her eyeline.

At the door the rector turned and for the last time addressed the congregation. 'I am the resurrection and the life, saith the Lord: he that believeth in me, though he were dead yet shall he live; and whoever liveth and believeth in me shall never die.'

Magic, she thought, pure magic; if only I could believe it to be true how lucky I would be.

By the time they got out of the church the coffin had been placed in the hearse and the door shut. The wind was cold and people huddled beneath their umbrellas in a dispirited way. She made her way over to the brother who was standing apart.

'I'm Henry's ... umm. I'm Stephanie O'Connor.' She took his hand. 'I'm really sorry for your trouble.'

'You're very good to have come.' He held her hand. 'I'll be going in to see Henry tomorrow. When all this is over. How is he?'

'He's not too bad, considering. I think he'll be all right. I'm sure he will be glad to see you.'

He gave a wry smile.

'We'll see. Thank you for coming . . . and the rose. That was a good thought.'

He turned abruptly to George with his hand outstretched.

George mumbled something that she couldn't hear and the pair of them set off down the hill towards the car.

'What a beautiful man,' she said after a moment.

'I suppose he is.'

'What's his name? Do you know?'

'Jeremy.'

She unlocked the car door. 'Hop in. Do you want a sleep first or will I bring you round to the hospital?'

'I think I'd better go and see Henry first. If I lie down I might sleep forever.'

The hearse edged slowly past them, followed by a green car driven by Jeremy. He raised a finger from the wheel in salutation as he passed them. They watched the tiny procession for a moment or two.

'Well, that's that,' said George. 'Sad enough.' He looked at her face. 'Sorry. But after all what can you say?'

'Sad enough,' repeated Stephanie.

She started the car.

'Do you think she did it on purpose?'

She didn't answer.

'Like, wanted them both to go together.'

'If that was what was in her mind she certainly didn't do a very good job.'

'I've wondered ever since I heard the news.'

'Who told you? I should have rung, I know, but then when he didn't seem so bad I thought I'd wait a while.'

'Tash, of course. Cried down the phone, bawled, screamed until I said I'd come, then she turned off the waterworks and was quite normal. If you could ever call her quite normal.'

Stephanie laughed.

'She can be such a pain. Anyway she didn't come to the funeral. She never took to Charlotte. She hasn't been to see Henry either. I think they had a furious falling out. You know how with Tash that can carry on for years. I expect they'll get together again now. After this . . . bereavement.' The rain seemed to be slackening off and there were some pale blue patches in the sky.

'Do you want a cup of coffee first?'

He shook his head.

'I think I'd rather just go and see him while I have the energy in my body.'

'I'll wait in the car park. You should see him on your own. Oh George, he will be so pleased to see you.'

George took out his handkerchief and mopped at his face.

'You think?'

'I know. Henry's not one for bearing grudges. You know that too. It doesn't matter what you said to him, George. That's all water under the bridge . . .'

'Hmmm. You are a very optimistic woman.'

'You're brothers.'

'A very sentimental point of view, if I may say so. Since when have brothers had to love each other, had to not hurt each other, had to forgive and forget? Since never.'

'I don't know what you fought about . . .'

'And I'm not going to tell you.'

'OK. That's fine by me.'

He rubbed his left hand with the handkerchief and then folded it and put it back into his pocket.

'When's the next book coming out?' he asked after a little while.

'God knows. I've got four or five more stories to write. It's a bit like getting treacle out of a treacle well.'

He laughed.

'Tell me, will you have him back?'

'Heavens, no. I've got sublimely used to living without a man constantly around. I love that freedom. I love being able to make my own decisions, I love being able and free to flirt, to have unpainful relationships. Once Ciara leaves school I'll be able to do exactly what I want.'

'Such as?'

'I might go and live in Tuscany, buy a little property and raise grapes.'

'I never knew you had such a thought in your head.'

'I don't. My point is that if I felt like doing it, I could do it. I could go into politics, get a seat in Dáil Éireann, I could become an actress, write a book, become a world-famous chef. Go into a convent.'

'Stop. I get the point. Don't you ever think about loneliness?'

'Do you?'

'Well, no, but—'

'Then why should I?'

He grimaced.

'No earthly reason.'

She took her eyes from the road for a moment and smiled at him.

'I do love him, you know, and I'm prepared to be his friend. A good friend . . . now that she's gone . . . I know I shouldn't say that . . . but live with him again? No. Anyway I bet you a million dollars he wouldn't want to come back to me. Bear that in mind.' She stared fixedly at the road ahead, at the cars splashing through puddles. 'I like him. Yep.'

'Not enough to . . . He's going to be very vulnerable for a time.'

'Look here George, you take him to Toronto, if you're so disturbed about him. I was vulnerable and he left me. I know you and Tash fought with him about that, but neither of you tried to move in with me. You didn't invite me to Toronto when he set off into the sunset. Did you?'

'Would you have come?'

'Of course not. He bloody broke my heart in smithereens, he hurt the kids. He's not coming back to live in the house again, and don't you dare offer it to him as a solution to his problems. Hear me? Hear me, George?'

'I hear you. Loud and clear.'

She turned sharply to the right and then again into the hospital car park. She drove him to the entrance. AMBULANCES ONLY was written in large letters on the ground.

'I've got shopping to do. I'll pick you up here in half an hour. OK?'

'OK.' He got out. He bent forward and shouted through the closed window. 'You're a great lady, know that?'

'Go to hell,' she shouted back and drove off.

∗　∗　∗

I opened my eyes and there he was.

George.

I closed them again and thought to myself, don't be such an idiot, George is in Toronto, and then gave myself a mark for remembering. Cautiously I opened my eyes again. He sat in my chair beside the bed leaning forward with an anxious look on his face.

'George,' I said. 'What on earth are you doing here? I'm not dying am I?'

He laughed, that old chuckle of a laugh, that fat man's laugh, that always made me feel so well each time I heard it.

'I had to come and make sure. Just one day, there's no time left any longer for sentimental gestures. A quick flash in and then out again and straight back to work. That's the North American continent for you. I'll come back though, bro, I'll spend my annual vac. here. I'd like to see you up and about again.'

He took my hand and squeezed it.

That was the moment that it all came flooding back into my mind again; well, not quite everything, but I became a man with a past, a real person, not just a forlorn patient. The accident and the time before it was still a black hole, but I remembered meeting her. Clean bright memories.

Her hand on my arm, her exquisite almond-shaped nails there shining pink against my black dinner jacket.

She smiled.

'I've come to say goodbye.'

'You have to say hello first.'

She put out her hand and touched my face. A brush of a touch, no more.

'Hello.'

She turned away into the crowd and moved towards the door. I started after her.

'Hey, wait, who are you?'

'Henry.'

Stephanie's voice.

Her dark hair was cut short like a man's.

'Henry.'

She raised her hand above her head and gave a little wave; whether it was a wave for me or someone else I couldn't tell.

'Henry.'

She was gone.

'Henry, darling. We're going. Do come on.'

George chattered on.

'Anyway, Steph is giving me a bed for the night and I go back first thing in the morning. At least I've seen you, bro. At least bridges are mended. Aren't they?'

'Yes. That was a ding-dong we had. I thought I might never see you again. You stormed out in such a passion.'

That laugh again.

'We, that is Steph and I, we went to the funeral.'

'Oh yes.'

'Just now. I've come from there. It was raining. It still is.' He jerked a thumb towards the window. 'Cats and dogs. I just made it. I really surprised Steph. She brought a rose, from you. I, ah, put it on the coffin for her. On her behalf . . . well really on your behalf. Yes, on your behalf.'

'Thanks. That was good of you.'

'We didn't go to the grave. We neither of us . . .'

'Were there many people there?'

'Not bad. We spoke to her brother.'

'Jeremy?'

'Yes.'

'Is he all right?'

'He seemed fine. Shocked, of course. Stunned might be the better word. He seemed a nice enough chap.'

'Yes.'

'He wanted us to go and sit with him, but we said no.'

'Would you ask Steph to bring me some books? Thrillers, easy reading stuff, she'll know what. She was always good like that.'

'He says he'll . . .'

'If she doesn't want to come herself one of the children can bring them.'

George stood up.

'Do you want me to go?'

'Don't be a fool, of course I don't want you to go. I want you to stay for weeks, just there. Be there always when I wake up. Protect me.'

'Protect you?'

'From myself.'

'Can't do that, bro. No one can do that.'

There was a long silence. Then he spoke again.

'Why do you think you need protecting from yourself?'

'Don't we all?'

'I don't, and I don't think you do either.'

'I am anxious. Maybe I will be surprised by my recollections. Upset, very alarmed. Maybe there's stuff in there I don't want to know about.'

'That'll make you just like the rest of us. Heads filled with secrets. You'll survive.'

'I need oranges.'

'I'll tell Steph.'

'An important part of my survival kit.'

My eyelids drooped. He touched my shoulder.

'I'll be off, bro. I'll keep in touch. Get well quickly. Bye.'

I grunted. I wanted to say goodbye. I wanted to thank him for coming, for being my brother, but all I could do was grunt.

Darkness. And in the darkness I heard his footsteps cross the room and the sigh of the door opening and closing and then the relentless rain falling.

*   *   *

She was standing outside the door waiting for him to come out, the umbrella over her head.

'They wouldn't let me park there. We're miles away. Would you like to wait in the porch and I'll come and collect you?'

'I'm fine. I can walk.'

He took her arm and they made their damp way through the cars.

'Everyone in Dublin seems to be here visiting. All trailing bugs and germs around the place. It's a noxious thought.'

'He wants oranges ... oh ... and thrillers.'

'That's not too complicated. How was he?'

'He looks grim, but he seemed pleased to see me. Genuinely. He can't take much conversation yet. He fell asleep.'

'He's probably on loads of painkillers.'

'I told him we went to the funeral.'

'What did he say?'

'Not much. At least he seemed to know that a funeral had happened.'

He took his handkerchief from his pocket and shook it and then wiped his face again.

'Tired?' she asked.

He nodded.

'You must get into bed when we get home and stay there. I'll bring you up your supper on a tray.'

He shook his head vehemently.

'No, no, no. I don't want coddling. I can sleep all day tomorrow on the plane. I suppose I should go and see Tash.'

'I'll ask her to dinner, then you won't have to go trailing all over town.'

'Now that is very kind.'

'If she comes.'

'She'll come all right. Yes. She'll come and she'll eat like a starving lion. I'm sure she doesn't eat proper meals on her own. Old people don't, you know. They pick at things. Eat out of tins, all that sort of stuff.'

'How do you know all that? You've been in Toronto for years.'

'I presume. I watch the box. I go to movies. I have friends with ageing parents. They all seem to follow the same pattern.'

'Tash isn't like any other ageing parent that I've ever come across.'

'I suppose she is quite remarkable.'

'She's working for another exhibition.'

'She has such energy.'

'For work, yes, for other things no. I suppose that's all that matters though. Here we are.'

She pressed the key and lights flashed in the car beside them. He opened the door and got in. 'It's going to be bloody rush hour. It'll take us hours to get home.' She slammed her door and started the engine.

*　*　*

Tash rolled up about eight o'clock in the evening. She tripped into the house, over a long purple scarf that had become detached from her neck and swung between her feet.

'Bloody hell,' she shouted as she hit the floor.

Stephanie wiped her hands on her apron and went out into the hall. Tash was on the floor, a bundle of brightly coloured wool, held together by a purple silk scarf.

'Are you hurt? What happened?' She leant over the old woman and took her by the shoulders.

'I tripped. Of course I'm not hurt, merely startled. Let go of me. I can get up without you pulling at me.'

She wriggled her shoulders; as she moved a delicate smell of drink rose in the air. Stephanie let go of her and stepped back, ready to offer a hand if it were needed. Tash struggled for a moment or two and then stood up. She bent and picked up the scarf which was on the floor and wound it three or four times round her neck.

'Hello dear,' she said to Stephanie, holding out her cheek for a kiss. 'Where's the boy?'

Her cheek was soft and powdery.

'Upstairs. I hope he hasn't fallen asleep.'

'Ah haha. Why would he do a thing like that?'

'He came from Toronto, Tash. He only arrived just in time for the funeral.'

'Oh that.' She walked slowly towards the sitting room door; Stephanie watched her. 'Have you a drink, darling? I'd murder for a drink. I've had a fierce day.' She went through the door and her voice floated back into the hall. 'Whiskey if possible. But I will accept a glass of wine if that's all you've got. I must not stay up too late. That's what the doctor said to me the last time I saw him. Did you know I had been seeing the doctor? I will go at half past ten. It really is in spite of my better judgement. He treats me as if I were a teenager. I have stopped going to see him now, but I will still leave at half past ten.'

Stephanie followed her into the room, where she was prowling round like some huge caged animal. She took off her hat and threw it onto a chair and then unwound the scarf and threw it after the hat.

'You'd better wake him up, you know. There's no point in my coming if I don't get to see him. Yoo-hoo, George.' She dashed to the door and called again. 'George. Hey boy.'

Calmly Stephanie poured whiskeys for both of them. There was a thud from upstairs. Tash came back into the room.

'That's him electrified. Thanks dear.' She took the offered glass and took a long drink. 'That's good. That's necessary. First today.' She raised her glass towards her daughter-in-law. Stephanie laughed. 'Laugh away. It's my first strong drink today. I've made out with wine. That was another boring thing the doctor said, no whiskey. I have cut down a bit, but I don't get the same buzz from wine. It seems to me that at eighty whatever it is I am I should be able to drink the sea dry, if I want to.'

Footsteps on the stairs and the sound of George's slightly wheezy breath.

'That's my boy.'

She took another drink and turned towards the door. George came in, looking crumpled and sleepy. She took a step backwards and looked him up and down.

'My dear George,' she said. 'You look like something the cat brought in.'

'The poor man's exhausted. Don't be so terrible to him. Drink, George?'

'Thanks. Good evening, Tash.'

He moved towards her and kissed her cheek. For a moment she held his shoulder and then seemed to push him away.

'Why has it been so long? Old. You look old. Can I have a son as old as you? Oh God. Why aren't you staying with me?' She threw herself on the sofa and put her feet up. 'Hey? Why?'

Stephanie held a glass out towards George.

'I met him at the funeral, Tash. I invited him. It seemed the easiest thing to do. He's off again at the crack of dawn.'

'Work calls,' said George weakly. He took the glass from her hand and went and sat down beside his mother. They stared at each other quite inimically.

'You don't write,' said Tash.

'Neither do you.'

Stephanie fled to the kitchen and began to lay the table, clattering knives, forks and spoons, plates and dishes. She stirred the soup, she cut some bread. She heard their voices, the little runs and the pauses, no real rhythm of conversation, just flutters of question and answer, suppressed anger. She couldn't hear the words. She was glad of that. Tash was sometimes so warm and loving and then other times hateful and angry. She turned off the oven. She sang a little song in her head. She thought of Henry tucked up in his hospital bed.

'Do not ever, ever, ever ask that woman into this house again,' he had once said.

'She's your mother.'

'She is a scorpion, a gorilla, an angry Indian tiger looking for prey. I don't want to be eaten by my own mother. Lock the door when you see her coming. Lie on the floor and pretend there's no one here. Just don't bloody let her through the door.'

'You'll change your mind.'

'Never.'

Of course he had.

She had seen them not long after that running towards each other at Punchestown races, like lovers in some old movie, and catching each other in a warm and loving embrace. She had been so glad at that moment that her own parents had led dull, undemonstrative lives, courteous, calm and affectionate. No passion. Passion was not a good thing, she thought. Passion eats you up.

'Food,' she shouted and ladled soup into bowls.

'Where is the beautiful Ciara?' asked Tash as she sat down.

'Out with friends?'

'Have you seen her, George? She has the most wonderful hair. I can't think where it came from. No one in our family has ever had red hair.'

'No. I haven't seen her. I haven't seen either of the children.'

'I never see them. They never come to visit. Yes, they say. Yes, we'll be around next week and they never come.'

'That's not strictly true, Tash.'

'The boy is gay. Did you know that?'

George crumbled some bread into his soup. He cleared his throat.

'Donough. Gay. Nice, bright lad, but gay. As a bee. Not surprising really. When you come to think about it. Hey?'

She stared from one to the other, turning her head from side to side like a little bird.

'I do see him from time to time. He comes to my studio. He brings his nice young man with him. Have you seen their house, Steph?'

'Not yet, but—'

'Wonderful. Such good imaginative taste. I'm giving them a painting.'

'That's nice of you.'

Tash twiddled her fingers and, surprisingly, went a little pink.

'Yerss,' she said. 'There is nothing wrong with — people of the same sex loving each other.'

Stephanie and George spoke at the same time.

'Of course not,' said Stephanie.

He said, 'I never said there was.'

'Hhhmph,' said Tash and they all ate their soup in silence for a moment or two.

'And how is my beautiful granddaughter?' Tash asked. 'Have you seen her, George? No, of course you haven't. I asked you. Didn't I? Sometimes I think that maybe I'm going a little potty. You'll pop me in the funny farm when that happens? Hey, Steph, won't you?'

'You're being a little tiresome. You can be from time to time. They wouldn't have you, darling. You're going to have to stick it out to the end.'

Tash threw her head back and let out a giant cackle of a laugh. She put her hand on George's arm.

'It is so lovely to see you, George. I shall be good. From this moment on. I really shall,' and she gave him a sweet smile. 'I love you, darling.'

They all had some more soup.

'Now dear heart, you must tell me all about Toronto. Maybe I might like to come out and visit you. In the fall. That would be the right time to come, wouldn't it? I could get a lot of painting done in the fall. Do you have a garden?'

'Yes.'

'I could work in your garden for you. I could cook for you. And I could paint. Just a couple of weeks. We could become reacquainted. Couldn't we?'

'We could indeed. What a great notion, Tash. I will look forward to your visit enormously.'

'I really feel I have neglected my children. People always say that when they grow up they don't need you any more. I don't think that is true. No. No.' She pushed her soup bowl away.

'Lovely soup, my darling. Do you feel you need me, George? Tell me honestly.'

'Umm,' said George.

She put out a hand and touched his arm.

'Don't bother,' she said. 'Silly question. I really hate travelling. So . . .' She smiled, a strange, big all-embracing smile. 'So, I'll say no now, this moment, to your invitation. Mind you I am tempted by the notion of the fall. All those wonderful rampaging colours.'

'I don't think you should say no, not as a final answer. Let it hang a while, Tash.'

Tash touched his arm again.

'Yes. I'll do that.' She took a drink from her glass. 'I must say I feel quite childless at times. How badly I must have brought you both up. What do you say to that?'

'Nothing, darling. I enjoyed being your child. We had much more fun than any of our friends. Moments of deep embarrassment, and, of course, anger, but a lot of fun. I think I would speak for both of us.'

'I wouldn't do that if I were you.'

Stephanie laughed and began to collect the soup bowls. She carried them over to the sink.

'I think he could do that all right. I think that Henry would feel the same.'

'I always wanted a girl.' As she spoke Tash squeaked her finger round the rim of her empty glass. 'Each time there was this awful slash of disappointment. Not, of course,' she stared into George's face, 'that it lasted long. Just a pang. You know, a twinge. I think that was your father's fault. He had no girls in him. I think I'll have another little drink, dear.'

Stephanie paid no attention to her request; she wrapped her hands in a dishcloth and lifted a casserole out of the oven.

'Wine,' suggested George, pushing the bottle towards his mother. She sighed and helped herself.

'He was such a sweet child.'

'Who?'

'Henry, of course. Much more charming than you. You were a grump. I said to your father, no one must shorten their names. If I'd wanted him to be called Harry, I'd have called him Harry. You can't mess about with George, can you?'

'I don't suppose so.'

'He was so pretty.'

'He's alive, Tash. You're pushing him into the past. Here.' Stephanie put a plate of food down in front of Tash. 'Eat that while it's hot.'

'That's too much, dear. I have no appetite these days. Half of that'll do me. Quarter.'

'Leave what you don't want.'

'I'm starving,' said George. 'I feel as if I hadn't eaten for a week.'

'Do you do your own cooking?'

'Of course.'

His mother cackled for a moment and then picked up her knife and fork.

'I bet it isn't as good as this. Stephanie is a wonderful cook. Henry didn't know how lucky—'

'Tash!' Stephanie put a plate down in front of George. 'Just shut up. You're being ghastly. Eat your food and shut up.',

There was a long silence. Stephanie sat down and began to eat. George poured her some wine. Tash looked angry.

'I shouldn't have come,' she muttered. 'I should not have come. No. More wine? Yes. George, pour me another drop while you're at it. Why do you all hate me so much? That's what I would like to know. What have I ever . . . yes. I was a terrible mother. I know. I knew at the time. I was not born to be a mother. I am an artist. Even now, in my declining years. My painting always comes . . .'

'What time is your plane, George?'

'. . . first. I love my children, nobody can argue with that, but I never . . .'

'Nine. I have to get to London then . . .'

'. . . never let them stand between me and my work. I lived . . .'

'I'll drive you out.'

'. . . to work.'

'No, no, no. I couldn't possibly let you do that. I have to be there by eight.'

'I'll drive you out. It's no problem.'

'I . . .'

'Don't let's argue, George dear. I so seldom see you. It would be a great pleasure to drive you out.'

'No one can argue that I have worked all my life. Sixteen I was when I went to the College of Art. A child, you might have thought, but luckily my parents recognised my talent and so did the—'

'Tash.' Stephanie spoke the name sharply. 'We do know, really we do, all about you. And we all love you to bits. You know that. The boys, me and the children. We're all crazy about you.'

'How sweet you are.'

'Thank you. George, talk now. Tell us about your life, about Canada, quick quick before she gets going again.'

George laughed.

Tash refilled her glass and spilled some wine on the table as she did so. She began to mop at it with her napkin.

'Oh dear, oh dear oh dear.'

'That's all right, Tash, don't worry.'

And George started to talk.

He didn't draw breath; his voice swooped and flew, little coughs filled the gaps in his talking, and his head nodded and bobbed. He told them about Toronto and the lake and the longest street in the world and the restaurant on top of the tower that revolved as you ate, about his neighbours and colleagues, about the woman he had almost married but how he had decided not to at the eleventh hour, second really, how lonely he had been at moments, how he went to New York once a month to see plays and hear music, and Montreal had more charm but Toronto was where the money lay and moved; it was where you had to be, a truly multicultural city. Cough, cough, cough. He told them about the maple forests and the scorching summers and how cold it was in the winter, about the St Lawrence seaway and the maritime states, and the museum with the huge room full of Henry Moores. It didn't seem as if he would ever stop until Stephanie put out a hand and touched his arm and pointed to Tash who lay back in her chair fast asleep, her mouth open and a little drip of spit running slowly down her chin.

'I bored her to sleep.'

'Alcohol rather than you.'

George shook his head.

'I've always bored her. She used to yawn when I started to talk. Opened her mouth really wide, I could see almost all the way down her throat. She never did that with Henry, only me. I grew up feeling I was the world's great bore.'

'You escaped.'

'Canada's full of bores; they don't notice me there.'

Stephanie laughed.

'They bore in two languages there. God, how mean of me to say that. They are so nice.'

'So are you. But you know that.'

'She never thought so.'

'Henry always thought she disliked him too.'

'She was always in behind that big door, across the yard. It was too heavy for us to push it open. We never saw her. She used to smell of turpentine. I remember that we would smell turpentine and then she would appear, magically.'

'I did not.' Tash's eyes popped open. 'I never smelt of turp ... turp ... Give me a napkin. I have dribbled on my chin. God, oh God how I hate being old. One day, I know, you'll lock me up, put me away in some sort of home. But, and I say but now to you, if I get wind of your intentions I will kill myself first. I will do that. I have the means. Don't think I haven't. I have the means.'

Stephanie wiped her chin gently.

'Nothing on earth would make any of us do such a thing.'

'Ha, ha haha,' the old woman cackled. 'That's what they all say.'

'Come on. Come on now, Tash. I'll drop you home. George needs to get to bed.'

'No need. Mr Cook is waiting outside.'

'Not all this time, Tash. The poor man. He'll be frozen. He'll be starving.'

'I pay him well. I don't know what I'd do without him. Give me another glass of wine and then I'll go.'

'It's all gone.'

'Well then, I suppose there's nothing to keep me here.' Her eyes roamed round the room, passing with a certain speed over her son. She pushed herself to her feet; the table quivered as she grasped its edge. 'I will go and see the boy in hospital. Not just yet. I will give him some recovery days. Next week. You may tell him that I will come next week. Yes. If you go. Personally I wouldn't go if I were you. No, I would not. Lovely dinner my dear. You must come to me, next. I will give you a tinkle, *un petit coup de téléphone.*' She picked up her scarf and wrapped herself in it. She walked across the room; at the door she stopped and turned towards George. 'Never you fear my lad. I will come. I promise you that. I will have an exhibition in Toronto. You must send me the names of some galleries. Good galleries.'

She waved a corner of her scarf towards them and was gone.

Stephanie got quickly up from her chair and went after her. George put his head in his hands and laughed and then suddenly found, to his surprise, that he was crying, hot tears bursting out from under his fingers.

'It's all right. Dear George, it's all right.'

'I'm just tired. That's all. No problem, Steph, no problem.' He groped with a hand for a handkerchief, finally pulling one from his trousers pocket. He rubbed at his face, he blew his nose. He looked up towards where she was standing, her face distressed for him. He shook his head, he smiled a painful smile. 'Yes,' he said. He didn't know why.

She put her hand out and touched his shoulder.

'Dear George.'

'I must come back more often.'

'You must. Absolutely. We'd like that. We really would. Promise me you'll do that.'

He nodded his head.

'She drinks a lot, doesn't she? Too much. I think. Yes.'

'She's over eighty, George. As she says she can drink as much as she likes. And smoke, take drugs, ballroom dance. I guess when you get to eighty you can do what you like.'

'I suppose you're right.'

'And she's still painting, with such energy. I bet you she'll have an exhibition in Toronto and sell the lot.'

He laughed.

'Have another drink?'

He shook his head.

'Bed.'

'A cup of tea?'

'No. Nothing. I must go to bed.'

'OK. I'll call you at half past six. We should leave by seven.'

He stood up and leaning towards her kissed her cheek. His lips lingered for a moment.

'You're a great lady, Steph. You know—'

She pushed him away gently.

'I know. Go to bed, before you say something stupid.'

'It wouldn't be stupid, just truth . . .'

'Go. Goodnight. Sleep well.'

'You know I nearly came back when I heard that . . . he'd . . . well, gone.'

'Yes. But you didn't.'

He shook his head.

'No. I thought you wouldn't thank me. I thought——'

'Go to bed. Please, George.'

He raised his hands miserably in the air and moved towards the door.

'He always won,' he said as he disappeared.

*   *   *

Better weather.

Blowy, but no longer grey.

I can see the bare branches dancing in the wind.

I can hear the occasional gust and the window rattles now and again.

I am in my chair, padded with white pillows. The pain is not so bad today; my shoulder throbs and something bangs from time to time in my head.

I did not dream last night; my sleep was deep and without the disturbing faces and voices that have been haunting me.

A lady came round with books on a cart. Nothing to write home about, but I picked out a couple of thrillers from amongst the Cecelia Aherns and Jilly Coopers that most people seemed to want; nothing too heavy to hold or to digest. The lady smiled at me and said she'd be back the day after tomorrow and she would try to bring something that I would really like. I thanked her politely. I think it's pretty unlikely.

I would like George to come back.

I could sit here in my chair padded with white pillows and shut my eyes and he could talk my past to me, and my memory would seep back. That would give me comfort. This time I would listen, I would not allow my attention to be distracted by ghosts.

Outside in the passage I can hear the pattering of feet; there is seldom silence, sometimes the squeak of a wheel on the polished floor and a murmur of voices. That is the way I like it to be. I wonder have I always been like this.

It is frightening to have no past, but it will come back. I do feel stirrings in the mist.

My eyelids droop, not even the distractions of Patricia Cornwell can keep them open.

No dreams, only blackness. No spectres, calm blackness. Calm.

He must have come in while I slept. When I opened my eyes he was standing by the window, quite gilded by the autumnal sunlight. He looked melancholy.

Jeremy. I thought the name. I swear I didn't speak it, but he turned towards me just the same.

'Henry.'

He seemed to run across the room and bent over me. He picked up my good hand and kissed it, then he held it to his warm cheek.

'Dearest Henry.'

'I'm all right you know. I'm not going to die. So they say.'

'Of course you're not going to die.'

He let go of my hand and stood up straight.

'I didn't know what to bring you, so I brought nothing, but next time ... next time ...'

'Jeremy?'

'That's my name.'

'Yes ...'

He pulled up a chair and sat down facing me; our knees were almost touching.

'You've heard that she's dead?'

'I ...'

'That she ... that she ...'

'No. I know nothing. I know that she's dead, but nothing more. Except of course about my own sorry state. Everyone's being very cagey. Will you tell me?'

There was a long pause. Jeremy's hands were clasped in his lap; he stared at them.

'Yes. I suppose I should,' he said at last. 'Otherwise ... well ... I suppose I should. I ...' He stopped speaking and scratched at his nose with a thumb. 'She was so angry.'

Maybe this was going to be too much for me, I thought; the beating in my head had become fretful and I longed to close my eyes.

'Angry?'

He nodded.

'Angry.' He muttered the word.

It buzzed in my head like a fly on a window pane, and the beating went on.

He continued to scratch at his nose. It didn't seem as if he were about to speak.

'Charlotte,' I said. 'I presume you're talking about her?'

He nodded.

'We have to get these things straight.'

He nodded again.

'Yes. You see ... it's really my fault. The whole thing. It never occurred to me ...'

He stopped speaking and stared at me.

'Just tell me.'

He began to cry; large tears rolled down his cheeks and splashed over his chin and down onto the pullover that he was wearing. This was too much, I felt. But then ...

He pulled a handkerchief from his trousers pocket and began to mop at his face.

'I'm sorry.'

The tears came on, thick and fast.

She was after all his sister. That was correct. Was it not? He had every right to cry about his sister's death.

He blew his nose. He got up from the chair and went over to the basin, turned on the cold tap and splashed his face with water. He lifted his head and stared at himself in the mirror above the basin, then he groped for the towel and dried his face. He turned towards me, I didn't want to hear what he had to say. He looked at me over the top of the towel; his eyes were enlarged with tears.

'You see, I told her.'

'Told her what, for heaven's sake?'

He dropped the towel to the floor.

'That morning. You were out somewhere and she was going to fetch you and I ... arrived and she was there alone and I ...

I don't know why. I was so happy when I went into the house. I had no intention, none at all, I promise you that. I've always told her everything. Every tiny thing that's happened in my life, and of course enormous . . .' He walked slowly towards me as he spoke. 'Wonderful things too and she's always understood and I thought, I have to tell her this.' He stopped. I thought he was going to cry again, but he just stood looking down at me. 'I must have been mad. Yes. It all just burst out of me in a torrent of happiness. Can you understand that?'

'No. I haven't the faintest idea what you're talking about. Come on, calm down. Sit here.' I patted the bed. 'Just pause a moment or two and pull your wits together and then tell me what this is all about.'

He perched on the bed; I could see him trembling. I put out my good hand and took hold of one of his and held it.

'Come on,' I said. 'Spit it out.'

He nodded. We remained silent for a few moments.

'About us,' he said eventually. 'And she just flew off the handle.'

'Us?'

'Yes. I knew we were going to have to tell her some time. Sooner or later and so I just blurted it out. Sooner. I said that to myself. Sooner. I thought she was going to kill me. Instead she—'

'It was an accident.'

'No. Didn't she say anything to you at all?'

I couldn't remember. I strained at my mind. I closed my eyes, but I couldn't even see her face, let alone hear words.

'It was not an accident. I know. It was all my fault. I think she wanted to kill you both.'

'Stop.' I held up my good hand like a policeman on point duty.

'No. Now I've started I must go on.'

'I don't want to hear you.'

'You must. Anyway you must try. Even in dribs and drabs. Listen. You must listen to me.' He took my outstretched hand and crushed my fingers together; held it like that, tight.

'That night. OK, OK, maybe you don't remember that night. For God's sake, man, it was only three weeks ago. We were in that car. The same car. You were driving and suddenly you stopped. Remember?'

I said nothing. What could I say?

'You pulled over to the sea wall. Howth was dotted with lights and all the lighthouses were flashing, the South Wall, Howth, Dun Laoghaire, we could see them all. Each one with its own rhythm. Do you remember?'

I shook my head.

'I am trying to paint it for you. We don't often see stars now in cities, but the sky was all soft with them and the tide was out. It looked as if you could walk clear across the bay. I . . . I put my arm around you and leant my head on your shoulder and we sat warm and happy, at least I was happy, and stared out across the sea wall. There was no one about, not even a man with a dog.'

I felt the warmth and the peace of the scene creeping into me. I caught a glimpse of the lights flashing, end to end of the bay and I suddenly heard the distant whistle of a train.

'After a long time, fifteen, twenty minutes I said, Henry, what are we going to do? and you sighed.'

I sighed then, a long and melancholic sigh.

'Yes. You do remember, just like that, a deep sigh and then you said, We'll tell her. We have to do that. And then I'll move out of her life. We'll tell her soon. That is only fair ... You paused for a long while and then said: It will be difficult, but it is what must be done. You must remember.'

The words echoed for a moment in my head. I had rolled down the window of the car.

'I rolled down the window of the car,' I said and his face lit up.

'Yes. You did that. I don't know why, but yes.'

'I needed air.'

I breathed in the slightly salty air.

'Are you sure?' I asked him.

'Yes. Oh yes, Henry, I am so sure. No more nonsense. No more messing about, oh God, man, I am so sure.'

'And I.'

I opened the door and jumped out of the car.

'Come on.'

He looked startled.

'Where?'

'On the movies they always run when they're happy. It's an amazing filmic sign of happiness. I'm going to run.'

I ran down the steps onto the sand and I could hear his footsteps running behind me. I ran out towards the sea, splashing from time to time through small rivulets of shallow water. I remember not caring about wet feet or trousers or anything at all and I had run, my head full of stars, until it hurt me to run any more and I was nearly at the edge of the sea. I could hear its whispering. I stopped and he stopped just behind and we were panting, our lungs bursting, and we turned to each other and threw our arms around each other and just stood, our hearts drumming inside us. I started to laugh.

'Lord, what fools these mortals be.'

'Motley's the only wear.'

'We will wear motley from now on. You and I.'

Then we laughed again and again, kissed and laughed some more and the sea came in with delicate splashings round our feet.

Yes, I remember now that night.

My wet feet were heavy as we walked back hand in hand towards the car. I felt like a young lover.

Three weeks ago.

The sky had been soft with stars.

Three weeks.

'So, I told her, that day. The day it happened. She was in the kitchen. She was about to go and fetch you from the gallery. I was crazy. Quite crazy and happy and I said that I loved you, that we were lovers, that we had decided to ... well ... come out, I suppose. I hate that expression, but it was the one I used and then I stupidly said that I hoped she understood.'

'That—'

'She had listened with such care to what I was saying. She had her head bent towards me, in the way she had. She listened with her eyes as well as her ears.'

He rubbed at his face with his hand.

'She began to hit at me with her fists and scream ... get out of here you fucking bastard ... nothing more rational or measured than that ... out out out ... over and over again.'

'And you?'

'Well, I ran. I picked up my coat and ran out the door. I knew

71

her too well to argue with her, to try to make her see reason, not when she was like that.'

'Love is not reasonable.'

I wondered as I said the words how I knew.

'I skulked about in the garden. I had to see her again. After all ... she's ... was ... my sis ... I should have left it to you. Anyway I skulked and it started to rain and I stood under that chestnut near the gate and I thought well hell, she'll calm down. She'll take this in her stride. Everything will be OK. It will. I really talked myself into believing that.'

There was a long silence between us, then he slowly stood up.

'She was my sister. I loved her. Yes. I don't know why I did such a terrible thing. Now. She's gone and you—'

'I'm here. I'm going to be OK. They keep telling me that. You've just told me that ... my wife tried to murder me.'

'Oh no ...'

'Oh yes. That's what you said.'

'She killed herself. I don't know whether she meant ... I don't even know if she meant to kill herself or just frighten you.'

'I'm tired.'

'Yes. I'm going.'

He stood there.

'You see I just fall asleep, without warning.'

'Will I come back?'

'Of course. Tomorrow. Things will be clearer then. Little by little they get ... Don't be ...'

He put out his hand and touched my face. I knew him, I knew I loved him. I tried to smile at him but I must have fallen asleep.

* * *

Stephanie leant forward and switched on Lyric FM, then she rummaged in her bag for a peppermint. Damn, bloody rush hour. The man in the car to her right was drinking coffee from a plastic container; the steam rose round his face, his eyes drooped. I should have put George in a taxi, she thought. This is crazy. I could be here, just north of Drumcondra, forever. Not funny.

George wasn't funny either.

Pathetic really.

But nice, definitely nice.

'I have always liked George.' She said the words out loud, directing them towards the man drinking coffee. He tapped his fingers on the steering wheel. He was going to be late for work, she thought.

The car in front jerked itself on for about five yards, she jerked after it. *There is a lady sweet and kind* . . . sang a voice on the radio . . . *was never face so pleased my mind* . . .

He was always trailing along behind, there were times when she had wondered if he were going to come on the honeymoon with them . . .

I did but see her passing by . . .

Theatres, cinemas, bathing, picnics, climbing the Sugar Loaf, the races, all those cheerful courting things they had done there was George too.

. . . *and yet I love her*

till I die . . .

He was the most mournful best man she had ever come across. And she remembered she did have a small pang of guilt as they had waved him goodbye at the airport. From time to time she had wondered what Henry had been thinking at that moment.

The man to her right balanced his plastic beaker on his knee and his car whizzed forward about twenty yards.

Why am I always in the wrong lane?

. . . Her gestures, motions and her smiles . . .

Was marrying Henry getting in the wrong lane too?

Looks like it.

. . . her with her voice, my heart beguiles . . .

Yes we had a fine time, a wonderful time, until she came along, beguiling.

. . . I did but see her passing by, and yet I love her till . . .

With such speed, her beguiling. A matter of weeks. She had him out of our house and into hers. Lock, stock and barrel.

Another few yards of jerking. Red light flashed on, off, on again in the car in front, a bus swished past in the bus lane; she was momentarily tempted to follow it.

George.

There's no use you making sheep's eyes at me, George.

Tash is right, it would be like living with Henry's ghost. I'm better off on my own. For God's sake have I not discovered that in the last couple of years?

Yes. I have.

A woman's voice was being wholesome about music. A pleasing voice, lulling.

I may just go to sleep if this traffic doesn't move. Her voice should not be so soothing.

Next to her now in place of the man with the coffee was another man, talking feverishly into his mobile. He was also tapping with his fingers on the steering wheel.

Suddenly, for no apparent reason, her lane moved forward at speed, away from the mobile man and then past the man with the coffee. She smiled towards him as she passed, right on past the lights at Drumcondra village and down the hill towards the turn-off to the toll bridge. Are we flying now?

We are.

George.

His last words to her had been in a slightly mewing voice.

'Think about me, Steph. I think about you all the time.' A lie, of course.

She had taken his hand and smiled at him, a warm and loving smile that she knew how to do well.

He kissed her hand. He had held it to his cheek and she had been saved from saying anything that might have upset him by the disembodied airport voice begging all passengers for London to go straight away to their boarding gate.

'This flight is now boarding.'

'Goodbye George.' She rescued her hand. 'Come back soon.'

He turned and left.

She had watched him for a moment or two; he walked almost like an old man, his shoulders drooped and one foot shuffling a little. It's too early, dear George, for you to be starting to disintegrate.

Poor dear George.

Such a sweet ass.

She giggled as she said that.

The lights in the car in front flashed and they all stopped again.

Such a sweet ass.

She wondered if he would have been beguiled by Charlotte's sweetness.

No.

He would love her till death.

That was the sort of him.

The lights turned green and she slipped round the corner and there was free road in front of her. She put her foot cautiously on the accelerator.

'Who the hell was that?'

'Who?' asked Henry.

'That woman you were following.'

Her voice had been a little querulous, that had embarrassed her. She had felt her face getting red. Her face felt red now just with the thought of it.

He laughed.

'I wasn't following anyone.'

'Well who was the woman you weren't following?'

'I haven't the foggiest idea. I never saw her before in my life and I'll probably never see her again.' He had put his fingers on the back of her neck and gently stroked it and she remembered the shiver that had gone right through her body.

Had it been a premonition?

Or just pleasure at the touch of his fingers?

Lying fingers.

The shiver repeated itself, starting at the nape of her neck and twisting its way down her spine, dancing, twirling, now hot now cold. Even her foot was shaking as she pressed down the accelerator.

At least he's alive.

Ciara must go and see him.

I must be firm about that.

Books, pyjamas, fruit.

Yes.

And I suppose I should wash his clothes. No harm in that.

Yes.

The car in front stopped.

Stephanie stopped and behind her all those other cars, vans, lorries stopped and they all sat, pulsating in the dusty city air.

✳   ✳   ✳

It was all right.

He had touched my face.

Had he said he loved me?

I really needed someone to love me. Jeremy.

Such a name.

Such love his mother must have put into the choosing of it.

For me.

'Jeremy.'

I said it aloud and the nurse's voice answered.

'You're awake.'

She leant over me and smiled.

'That's good. The doctor will be round soon and we must give you a bit of a wash. Would you like a cup of tea now, or after?'

She pumped the back of the bed up as she spoke.

'Let's get clean first.'

'That's the ticket. We'll give you a nice wash and then you can get into your chair and I will make the bed. Everything will be shipshape and Bristol fashion for the doctor.'

She rolled towels around me, over the pillows and mattress. She was deft and I rolled as she pushed me and gently pulled me with her cool hands.

'Who's Jeremy?' she asked.

I felt my face going red.

'A friend.'

She handed me a toothbrush. 'Gently does it, and spit in the bowl. Now give your face a good wipe.' She took the toothbrush from my hand and replaced it with a face flannel warm and squeezed and smelling faintly of sweet soap. 'That's a good boy.' She worked with another flannel, soap, warm water, she hummed a tune as she washed me, a slightly mournful tune. My skin when washed felt fresh. 'Do you feel better now? A clean-up is a great help. Now let's pop on your PJs and you'll look like a film star.'

Soon I was sitting in my chair clean and feeling polished; even my hair had been combed; there could be no complaints from the doctor.

My mind seemed alert; ready, I felt, to cope with whatever lurking surprises the day might have in store for me.

I sipped at my tea and thought about what Jeremy had told me; it was hard to believe that she had wanted to kill me. I could understand someone wanting to end his own life. I could recollect the dark curtains that had sometimes imprisoned me as a young man, when the only escape seemed to be death. I used to lie in my bed and long for death to come, to pull the curtains away and let me be free.

I had told Tash one afternoon in her studio that I truly wanted to die. She had continued to paint and I sat in a chair and watched her in silence. I had wondered if she had heard what I had said to her. It had all seemed so important to me, so terrifying, I thought she should feel the same, but she just continued painting and I sat and stared at her back, both of us quite silent. After a long time she had begun to clean her brushes and stand them in the pottery jugs that clustered on the table by her easel.

'How selfish you are,' she said suddenly. 'Such thoughts are pure selfishness. Not to be handed round to other people. You mustn't burden other people with the dirt and fantasy in your head.' She put her brush down on the table and turned to me, her face furious. 'Why should I have to worry about whether you want to kill yourself or not? Why? Haven't I enough worries of my own? Now you hand me this . . . present! Well I don't want it. I shall tear it out of my head. I shall throw it out of the window. If you have such ridiculous thoughts in your head, son, keep them to yourself in future.' She rushed out of the room.

I laughed at the memory. She had always been so dramatic.

My ribs hurt.

I must not laugh.

My desire for self-annihilation had faded.

There was a cough. My eyes must have closed as I had thought about Tash. I opened them and she was standing there before me.

'Yes,' she said. 'You look pretty grim. I promised Stephanie that I would come.'

'Tash.'

'I brought you a bottle of whiskey.' She plonked a paper bag on the table beside me. 'Even if they won't let you drink it, you can give it to your guests.'

She stared at my face.

'Thanks,' I said.

Her eyes moved down my body.

'Well she didn't kill you. That's something, anyway. Are you in great pain?'

'From time to time. They give me—'

She nodded.

'I told you not to get mixed up with her. Didn't I? Didn't I?'

'Yes.'

'You remember.'

'A lot of our conversations are memorable.'

'Tcha.'

She approached the bed cautiously and perched on the edge of it like a bird on a branch. A little waft of alcohol drifted past my nose. I must have smiled.

'You can laugh.'

'I'm not laughing, Tash. Honest to God. Why would I laugh?'

'You and your brother seem to think of me as a comic character.'

'What rubbish.'

She turned her huge pale eyes towards me; she looked as if she were about to cry. I leant forward and took her hand.

'Dear Tash, you are such a magic person. Believe me George and I are in complete agreement on this one.'

'He looks so old now.'

'You saw him?'

'Last night, Stephanie asked me to dinner. I don't think

Canada agrees with him. He should be cheerful, married, a father. He's let all that slip away. Whereas you . . .' She stopped. She put her hand over her mouth for a moment.

'I?'

She shook her head.

'He always wanted Steph,' she said.

'I? What were you going to say about me?'

'Nothing.'

'She never looked at him. It was just as if he were a piece of furniture. He used to stand around staring at her with big sad eyes . . . your eyes, Tash . . . and I would say to myself, that's not how to do it, you idiot. She'll never look at you if you don't make her. If you don't spark her. She'll never love you like she loves me. So. I won.'

'You always won.'

'What were you going to say about me?'

'Wasn't it good of Steph to invite me to dinner? I wouldn't have seen George otherwise. It was such foolishness for him to come for one day only. He says he'll come again. I doubt it. He looks so old now.'

'Yes. You said.'

'I do repeat myself from time to time. Do you think this is the beginning of . . . you know what?'

'Darling, don't have such terrible thoughts. Of course it's not.'

'That's easy to say, but not to believe. As I have said to George and Steph, if either of you attempt to put me in a home, I have means of dealing with that. Yes, I have. You're looking flushed.'

'I'm supposed to keep calm, Tash.'

'You want me to go?'

'No, of course not. It's wonderful to see you.'

'A little drink.' She put her hand on the paper bag.

'No. It's a bit early for me.'

'I think it would calm me down. Just a little one.'

She flopped off the bed onto the floor and crossed the room to the basin. She took my toothbrush from its mug and threw it into the basin.

'Some people drink from the bottle ... or can ... I can't bring myself to do that. It's so ... well, unglamorous ... don't you think?' She removed the lid from the bottle and poured herself a good splash. She held the glass up in my direction. 'Mud in your eye.' She put the glass down on the basin. 'I was going to tell you about the motor accident that your father and I had, but I think I won't. I think I'll go.' She put the lid back on the bottle and put it back into its paper bag. 'When you're better. You must come to me when they let you out. I will mind you. Steph has too much to do. I will paint and I will mind you. That would be fun, wouldn't it? Just like all those years ago.' She slipped the paper bag into her coat pocket and headed for the door. 'I won't kiss you, darling. Germs, germs.'

'You never minded me, Tash.' I said it very quietly.

She turned towards me.

'I heard that. You always were an ungrateful little boy.'

She was gone. I heard her feet squeaking on the floor along the passage, a slow old woman's shuffle. I felt a heel. I also felt exhausted. I wanted to scream. I wanted to go home, but where now was my home?

In my whole life I had only ever had three homes; two

of them I could remember with clarity, the third, the most recent, veiled still, like an autumn morning with wispy scraps of mist.

She still lived in what had once been the coach house and stables of the house where we had lived as children. I remember the winter cold and the summer sun blazing in through the long windows. The apple trees, the espaliered pears and the plum trees buzzing with wasps. From the roof of the house, looking north, you could see the line of the sea and beyond it the lump of Howth Head and to the west the Dublin mountains in the distance. I can call back into my mind the sound of my father playing Beethoven on the piano, the notes creeping into my head as I sat upstairs doing my homework. I laid down my pen and closed my eyes. It was the Waldstein sonata and he played it well. He had strong fingers, my father, and I was able to imagine him pressing them hard down on the keys, squeezing the sound from the piano in such a way that a fourteen-year-old boy in the room above could hear and be happy. In such distant ways he had made me happy, whereas with her I had always felt anxious; I think that George did too, though we never spoke about it. Sometimes she had been so loving and kind; she would throw her arms around us, hug us, twist our hair in her fingers and tell us that she loved us to death. Other times we wouldn't see her for weeks; she would shut herself in her studio and if she caught sight of us she would turn the other way. I banged one day on her studio door. It was winter and I had run across the slimy cobblestones in the yard. I must have needed her desperately because I felt scared as I looked at my fist knocking on the door. It opened slowly and she stood there looking down at me. There was a smudge of red paint on the side of her nose. It had looked like blood.

'Yes.'

I can hear her voice now, unfriendly, cold.

Yes.

I can remember now what it was that had sent me slipping across the cobbles to her door.

Robert O' Carroll. What was it that we called him?

Something rude and crude, but it escapes me. Something schoolboyish, something simple, something that made us laugh each time we said it.

He was beautiful, he was seventeen, two years older than I was, he was captain of rugby, a hero in spite of the name we called him.

I must have been the last person to leave the changing room and he came from behind the door; he put a hand on my shoulder and nudged the door shut with his backside. He turned me towards him and held me close within his arms. He smelt of that awful soap we used in the school shower. I could feel the thudding of his heart and then my own, yes, my own was beating too. Very gently he took my chin in his fingers and turned my face up to his and kissed me. I remember now the softness of his mouth as it trembled on mine, I remember the feeling of his tongue squirming its way between my lips and I can remember the joy in my cock as it rose and then I punched him in the face and opening the door I ran down the stone passage till I was surrounded by noise and people and pushing and shoving and a master shouted, 'Quiet, boys,' and no one paid him any heed. I looked back down the passage and saw him standing at the door.

'A bit of quiet, please.'

He raised his hand and smiled.

My face, my neck, my whole body went red; I was drowning in the noise, my body shook with what seemed to be fear. I pulled my coat from the hook and ran home. I had to see my mother, I had to ask her; I had to have her stroke my head and say there there. Nothing is wrong, nothing my darling is wrong. I slipped on the slimy cobbles and the knee of my school flannels took on a green stain.

'Yes?'

I stood silently in front of her face.

'How many times have I told you not to come battering on this door. I am working. I must be allowed to work in peace.'

She turned back into the studio and banged the door in my face.

The next time I saw her she was as sweet as honey; she filled my pockets with tiny presents. I don't remember what they were, but it was something she always did to compensate in some way for her rejection of us. We as usual never mentioned what had passed; I never told her why I had come banging on her door. She never asked.

Robert.

Even as I sat there, half dreaming, propped in the chair by my hospital bed, I was warmed by the pleasure of thinking his name.

'Robert.'

Of saying it aloud.

'Robert.'

I spoke the name a little louder.

'Robert.'

The door opened and the nurse stuck her head round it.

'Everything all right?'

'Yes. Oh yes, thank you.'

She nodded and left.

It had become quite clear in my mind now, technicolour clear, and I remember only the happiness, like you only remember the sunny days of summer.

For two days we avoided each other, then I turned a corner at the top of the stairs and he was standing there, waiting, almost but not quite blocking my way.

I looked down at my feet. I could feel my face getting red; the rest of the school seemed to be rushing past me.

'I'm sorry.' His voice was low.

I nodded, all the time staring down at my shoes.

We stood quite still. Feet pounded past, shoulders bumped, voices became one huge blur of sound.

'Are your shoes so very interesting?'

A great wave of laughter surged up from my belly and I lifted my head. He was smiling at me. As I laughed I longed for him to kiss me again. He held his hand out towards me and I touched it. He laid his hand briefly on my shoulder and ran his thumbnail down the side of my neck. I nodded once more; it was the only thing I could do.

'Right so,' he said. 'That's OK then.' And he passed me and clattered down the stairs.

Everything was going to be all right.

Yes.

For two years we became best friends; we explored the world around us, we swam, we bicycled for miles into the Dublin mountains, and the Wicklow mountains. We lay on beds of pine needles in the darkness of woods and touched and stroked each other's bodies. His mouth became my mouth. I knew all its softnesses and intricacies; our bodies were like gardens which we loved and tended with care. We read the same books, we laughed at the same movies.

We fought, we made up. We talked through and round what seemed to us to be the important things in life. We fought again and yet again made up. He was the only person in the world who ever called me Harry.

'Harry.'

It was the day after my sixteenth birthday and we were sitting on the sea wall at Sandycove feeling exhausted and certainly for me a little hungover. It must have been a Saturday afternoon, as families and dogs moved past us along the pavement.

'Mmm?'

The sea splashed agreeably on the rocks beneath us and two children were fishing with nets. It was a good day, I thought, to have a hangover. It was a good day to be almost grown up.

'You're not listening. You're asleep. You'll fall off the wall.'

'I'm not asleep.'

'You know when term is over we're leaving?'

I looked at him. He was staring across the bay towards Howth.

'Immediately.'

'What?'

'The old man's got a Chair in Cambridge.'

'But I thought you were going to Trinity.'

'No.'

'Why not? You always said . . .'

'Cambridge. King's. It's all settled. The old man's old college.'

He always referred to his father as the old man.

'It's what they want me to do. They always have. Cambridge, nurturer of gods. That's the way they look at it. Mum was there too. She's not just a pretty face, my mum.'

'But . . .'

'No buts, Harry. Not a fucking but.'

He put up his hand between himself and the sun and I couldn't see his face but I knew by the trembling in his voice that he was very close to crying. We sat in silence for a long time and I thought how my joyful life was going to come to an end. All of a sudden he slithered down from the wall. He started to walk briskly along the footpath and turned to summon me with a jerk of his head. I followed him back to his house and up the granite steps to the front door. It was painted a sunny yellow. He took a key from his pocket and opened the door and we went into a long hall. The stairs were in front of us and halfway up a long window let the sunlight spill down into the hall.

'Yoo-hoo,' he shouted. There was no answer. The house was quite silent. Outside in the street a dog barked.

He took my hand and we went upstairs, past the tall window. His door had a china label on it. Robert, it said in blue squirly writing.

He opened the door and we went in. He walked across the room and pulled the curtains and we stood in the half light and looked at each other.

'We haven't done this,' he said.

I shook my head. I was excited and frightened at the same time. I couldn't speak.

He held out his arms. I couldn't move, I was trembling. He took me by the hand and led me to the bed. I sat and watched him undress.

'No one will come in.' He pulled off his second sock and stood quite naked in front of me.

Oh God, yes. I remember it now so well.

I remember the dim light, and a narrow streak of sunlight that split the room in two, his clothes a heap on the green carpet, and his bed which was more comfortable than mine and the two pillows that we tossed across the room and the dog in the street that barked again and again and the cars that hummed past. Again in the house there was silence. He came beside me and began fumbling with buttons and zips and I didn't stop him. I stood like some little prince while he undressed me and then pushed me down onto the bed.

'We have so little time,' he murmured into my ear. I said nothing. I held him fiercely. I held him so close that I hoped the imprint of his body would remain forever on mine. No time passed and all time passed and suddenly I heard a voice calling.

'Robert.'

I disentangled myself from him.

'Robert.' The voice was closer.

I scrambled from the bed and grabbed my shirt; I was shoving an arm into a sleeve when the door opened.

'Robert why oh why do I always have to——'

She stopped speaking and stared at me, ran her eyes insolently up and down my body and then she turned and left the room. She left the door open and I could hear her feet clicking on the stairs. A door slammed downstairs somewhere and then there was silence once more. I looked at Robert; he lay, hands behind his head, his legs splayed wide. He had a slight smile on his face.

'Don't panic,' he said. The smile flickered for a moment as he said the words. 'Don't panic.'

I remember so well now, my heart thudding and how my legs trembled as I ran down the stairs. She opened the drawing-room door as I came down the last flight and stood tall and angry there watching me.

'What a horrible little boy you are,' she said, as I crossed the hall. 'Luckily we are going, soon, very soon. Otherwise I would have to take this up with the school. But, I am going to ring your mother. Believe me, you sick little pervert, I have every intention of doing that.'

I was out into the air and the passing cars hummed and the dog was still barking and I ran until I had to stop because of a stitch in my side and I leant against a wall until it passed away. I was crying. I've always hated the word *pervert. Even now I want to scream when I hear someone use it, no matter what the context.*

I never discovered whether she had told my mother or not, but I suspect that she had; Tash used to give me knowing looks and winks and smile from time to time with a secret satisfaction. She loved the knowing of other people's secrets. Yes indeed she did. So here I sit in this hospital room broken in pieces and little by little the past is revealing itself to me. Things I want to know and things that might be better left unremembered.

The whole person.

How great it would be if you could only remember the good bits, the spiritual bits, the noble thoughts, the generosity, all the bits we hope for ourselves. Dreams, prayers, discard the blackness, let all the muck slide away.

Ah, yes, I remember it well.

I can't laugh. My ribs won't let me. But I can say ha ha ha. My eyes are drifting to sleep, so I can sleep with the sound of my own voice saying hahahahaha.

✳   ✳   ✳

Stephanie pulled the car into a small space in Mespil Road. She turned off the engine and put the key in her bag. She sat there. Two boys stood motionless on the grass verge of the canal, fishing rods in their hands, their schoolbags thrown under a tree; they seemed to be just willing the fish to attach themselves to their bait. Stephanie wondered if there were any fish in the canal and then wondered if they were edible and then wondered if it was worth skiving off from school to try to catch inedible fish. Probably was.

She looked back at Donough's house. Neat. Red front door and shining windows. A gravel path leading to the steps, traditional Irish granite steps with a curved iron railing on each side. There was a man standing at the window to the right of the hall door, with a cup of something or other in his hand; he was staring at her car. She sighed, opened the door and got out.

She reached into the back for the flowers she had brought from the garden. By the time she had gathered them from the seat and straightened herself up, the hall door was open and the young man stood on the steps. He waved his cup at her.

'You're just in time,' he called. 'The coffee's just made.'

'Good morning, Brendan. I hope you don't mind me dropping in like this.'

'Not at all my dear. It's lovely to see you and such scrumptious flowers.'

'It's a bit silly to bring flowers when you have painters in, but I couldn't resist picking them. There's not much in the garden at this time of year. I seem to be spending my time bringing people flowers at the moment. Alive and dead.'

He put an arm around her shoulder and drew her into the house.

The smell was of paint and coffee.

'You haven't been here before. Tash comes occasionally, drinks whatever whiskey there is about, blows a lot of kisses and staggers off. She has this tame taxi driver. It's no wonder she has to keep on painting.'

Stephanie laughed.

He brought her into a room on the right-hand side of the

hall. It was painted a wild canary yellow, no furniture, just two leather chairs. He put his cup on the mantelpiece.

'I'm just going to get your coffee. I won't be a tick.' He waved at a chair. Obediently she sat and he and the flowers left the room.

Why did I do this, she wondered? A question she was unable to answer. So she sat and listened to the sound of the workmen upstairs, a heavy footstep, a creaking board, a little rush of words and a laugh.

'Milk? Sugar?' called out Brendan's voice.

'Neither. I like it black.'

'Right you be.' He appeared back in the room with a mug held out towards her.

'Thank you.'

He took his coffee from the mantelpiece and sat in the second chair.

'Look,' he said. 'You're going to think me very rude, but I don't mean to be. I'm not going to show you round the house. I know Donough would want to do it himself and I haven't the foggiest idea where he is. He scrambled out and away at the crack of dawn. He may be back at any minute and he may not. Living in two houses is very complicated. It's going to be such a relief when the workmen are out and he can move his gear in properly. He'll be so pleased you dropped by.'

Carefully Stephanie balanced her mug on the arm of the chair.

'He only mentioned a couple of days ago that he was leaving. That he was . . .'

Brendan stared silently at her. Upstairs someone pulled a ladder across the floor.

'. . . leaving . . . that he was . . .'

Brendan still said nothing. After a moment or two he cleared his throat.

'He told me. He told me you weren't over the moon.'

'I was surprised. I was startled. He'd never said a word about leaving before. I'm delighted though, really I am, and it's such a lovely house. I just thought I'd come and have a quick look at it. See it for myself. I was just startled.'

He grinned.

'What a liar you are, Steph.'

'I'm his mother.'

'And I'm his lover.'

'Yes.'

'Why do you care?'

'This seems so permanent.'

'That's good. Most people think that's good.'

'I thought it was a passing phase. I thought—'

'He'd meet some nice girl and everything would be all right.'

'Something like that. I feel quite foolish. I feel why has this happened to me?'

'It hasn't happened to you. Nothing has happened to you.'

'I don't have any views about people being gay . . .'

'No?'

'No.' She shouted the word at him. 'I bloody don't. I never have. I just wish it wasn't him. How did it happen? Why?'

'Dear lady, you are being a little foolish. He was born that way. No one has done anything to cause it. It was the way he came out. One more little gay baby. Drink up your coffee, it will get cold. You'll get used to it. In a year or two you'll just wonder why you were upset.'

'I'm not really upset, I just wish things weren't this way.' She took a gulp of coffee. 'And by the way, it's nothing to do with you. I like you. I do.'

She stretched out her hand towards him. He took it.

'I like you too.' He raised his coffee towards her and she did the same. They looked like a right pair of idiots, and for a brief moment laughed, not catching each other's eyes, just idiots laughing.

'OK,' he said. 'It'll all be OK. You'll see. I'll mind him well.'

'I'm sure you will.' A rueful voice. She drained her mug and put it down on the floor. She stood up. 'I'd better go,' she said. 'Have you met Henry? No, no of course you haven't. Unless that's something else Donough hasn't told me.'

'I've never met Henry. Only Tash. Don't go. Stay a while. He may come back.'

She shook her head and moved towards the hall.

'One day he'll invite me. I will come then. I'm glad to have had a chat with you.' She gave a little wave and before he had time to stand up she had left the room and was out of the hall door. He got up and stood by the window watching her as she went down the steps. When she got to the gate she took her keys from the bag and pressed the button on her key ring. The car across the street winked at her. Brendan laughed and went to get himself some more coffee.

✳   ✳   ✳

Today Steph brought my little red-haired angel in to see me.

Why do I say little?

She's not little.

A beautiful young woman with hair the colour of copper beech leaves and huge green eyes.

A knockout.

I always knew she would be a knockout.

Another door into the past was opened when she came into the room. I remembered the pain of missing her. Each morning I would get up and know that she wasn't there, each morning I would think the pain would be less, but it never was.

Now, here I was, stuffed into the bloody chair, suffering a different sort of pain; grumpy, yes I was grumpy, I had nothing to read and my shoulder was aching. The door opened. I was expecting a nurse or doctor, an official of some sort. I glared at the opening door. I had nothing else to do and had no desire to arrange my face into some amiable design. Steph came in first, burdened with books and pyjamas, a pair of slippers and a box that looked as if it held a cake. I pulled my mouth into a smile.

'You look awful, but at least you're up. Good morning.'

She dumped the load in her arms on the table and came over to me.

'Good morning,' I said.

She bent and kissed the top of my head.

'Remember me?'

'Of course I do.'

'Let's see if you know who this one is. Come on in and close the door behind you.'

And in she came, cautiously, I do have to say, as if she didn't

know what kind of a freak she was going to see. She closed the
door as her mother had asked her to and stood beside it.

'Ciara.' I tried to get to my feet, but couldn't. I held out my
good arm towards her and she gave a little sob.

'My dear child.'

She ran towards me.

'Take care, he's damaged,' said her mother.

She landed in an ungraceful heap on the floor beside me and
took my outstretched hand and held it to her cheek.

'Ciara.'

'I feel so rotten.' I had to lean forward to hear the whispered
words. 'I didn't want to come and see you. Mum made me and
now . . . I've missed you so much. I never said it to anyone. Never
let on but . . .'

I put my hand on her head, I moved my fingers in her hair.

'It's OK baby. It's OK. Don't cry.'

'I have to.'

'It's uncool to cry.'

'It's pretty uncool to disappear for four years from your
family and then appear again in shreds.'

'I agree. I've missed you too, baby. Every day I've missed you.
Every day I have cried to myself because I've missed you.'

She looked up at me.

'True?'

'Really, really true.'

'May I kiss your face?'

'I couldn't think of anything I'd like more.'

'It looks so sore, so . . . beat up.'

'A kiss would make it better.'

We leant towards each other and her soft lips brushed my cheek. My eyes filled with tears. God, I thought, please don't let me cry. Please don't fucking well let me cry. Steph's voice stopped all thought of tears.

'Who wrote the script?' She had moved to the window and spoke the words over her shoulder towards us. 'There's not a dry eye in the house.'

'Moving reconciliation between father and daughter, school of *Now Voyager* 1942.'

She gave a little spurt of laughter.

'Memory coming back?'

'How could anyone who's seen it ever forget that film?'

'Mum, Dad, don't bicker.'

I pressed her fingers.

'We're not bickering, love, just testing waters.'

'Now you've seen us all, so you'll know us when we come in. We won't have any more anxiety. The ice is broken. Isn't that good? We can behave like a family again. I think that's scrumptious.'

She stood up; her eyes were shining with a strange light.

'I feel real again.' She twirled on her toes and looked as if she were going to dance. 'My life from now on will be so joyful.'

'Enough,' said Stephanie from the window. 'It's time you went to school. You've missed enough.'

'Must I?'

She looked from her mother to me.

'Of course you must. I said that before you came. Five minutes, I said, no more. You can come back again and again. Now, school.'

The girl looked at me and smiled.

I sighed.

'Much as I would love you to stay you'd better do what your mother says.'

'Bloody school.'

I nodded.

'Bloody school.'

'Goodbye Dad. For the moment. I'll be back so. We have so much reacquainting to do.' She leant down and kissed my cheek gently. 'Poor face,' she said. 'But you'll be better soon. We'll all be better soon.' And she was gone.

'What a lovely girl she is becoming.' I watched the door hoping that she might return.

'One might call her a proper little bridge builder.' Her voice was ironic.

'Have I done them a terrible damage?'

'I shouldn't think so, but they'll try and make you think so.'

'You've become a cynic.'

'No more than I've ever been.'

'You always used to speak your mind.'

'You remember?'

'I suppose I do. I think I remember being disconcerted by you.'

She laughed.

'That's good. I like that. The only time I could say you disconcerted me was when you left. I was convinced we were forever, till death us do part. I really believed in that fairy tale. I used to look at all those other people we knew splitting up, friends, relations, and think we'll never do that. We're good.

Then wham. Right out of the blue. Mind you, Tash used to tell me to enjoy what I had while I had it. Nothing lasts. She said I should have fought tooth and nail to keep you. Would that have been the right thing to do? She must have known something I didn't know. She never told me, even after you had gone. She raged at me.'

'Oh God, I'm sorry.'

'Sorry?'

'She can be so tiresome when she gets a notion into her head.'

'She's OK. She's alive and working. She's a great role model.'

'I'm not going to come back to the house, you know that don't you?'

'I bloody do. I wouldn't countenance that. Not for one second. That sort of want left me an age ago. God, I have freedom now and I wouldn't give it up for anyone. We can be friends though, and parents. The children will like that to happen. They have missed you, but they've been very brave and grown-up about the whole thing. Better than me. I kicked a lot of furniture to begin with. Then I began to like my own company. I suppose I was lucky.'

She held out a hand to me and I took it. It was warm and slightly rough; she pressed my fingers briefly and then took her hand away.

'I never stopped loving you, you know.'

She stood up.

'Don't say such a stupid thing. How the hell do you know? You don't remember loving me and you don't remember stopping loving me. Or why. That is what I want to know. Why? Why? Why?'

'I'll work on it.'

She gave a snort of laughter.

'You do that.'

Sweat was running down my forehead and my head was thumping.

She touched my shoulder.

'I'm off,' she said. 'Is there anything you need?'

'Oranges.'

'They're in the bag and some books. I remember your need for oranges.'

'Thanks.'

'Take care.'

She was gone.

Grey folds of sleep replaced her presence.

* * *

I find it so hard to stop sleeping.

Pain wakes me.

The need either for medication or to relieve myself.

Even the quiet footsteps of the nurses become part of my dreams.

I must haul myself out of this.

The moment any visitors I may have leave the room I slump back into sleep again.

I don't feel as if I were making any progress towards becoming a whole person once more, though I do have to say that my memory is finding itself in fits and starts. For instance I now know that I own a small publishing house out near the Phoenix Park. We publish poetry, small books of essays, memoirs, the odd biography, very few novels and only those of high quality. Far too many bad novels are published every year, and as publishers claw each other for more and more money the standard of writing falls.

I may of course have dreamt all this, but I don't think so. I remember walking in the park eating sandwiches during my lunch break, sitting on the steps of the obelisk watching mothers with small children and listening to the distant roaring of animals in the zoo. I remember as a boy riding in the park on Saturday afternoons with George. He was a better man on a horse than I was; he looked debonair and I think I looked nervous. I can see the deer moving among the trees and occasionally hear the bellow of a stag. The deer would raise their heads from cropping as we came near them and then, judging us to be harmless, would return to their eating once more.

Steph and I used to take the children to the zoo, presuming, in the way that parents do, that this was an enjoyable outing for them. I dreamt last night that I was walking along one of the paths holding Ciara's hand. Her hand was hot, almost feverish. I bent down and looked in her face. Tears were dragging their way down across her cheeks.

'Ciara, what's the matter? What's wrong, pet?'

We stopped walking and I crouched down beside her.

'Are you not feeling well?'

She began to sob.

'I hate it here.'

'But why, darling?'

'Hate it.' She yelled the words at me. 'Hate.'

She pulled her hand from mine and rubbed at her face.

'It's like a prison.'

'A prison? What an odd thought, darling.'

'All those poor animals. They're locked up, like in a prison. I hate it.'

I took her hand again and pulled her towards the restaurant.

'Come, darling. Come in here.'

'I want to go home.'

'Come on, silly billy. You can wait in here for me. I'll have to find Mummy and Donough. You'll be all right here. I'll get you a squash. You can just sit here and drink it. You'll feel better then.'

She nodded.

I gave her my handkerchief.

'Here. Wipe your eyes. Blow your nose. You do look a right mess.'

I pushed her into a chair and went to get her a drink.

'Keep an eye on her,' I muttered to the woman at the counter. 'She's a bit upset. I'm going to look for her mother.'

'Don't worry. She'll be all right. I'll keep her company for a few minutes.'

It was true, not really a dream, just a memory coming back into my head.

We took them home and never took them to the zoo again.

Steph was cross.

'Little Miss Brat,' she said later on that evening.

'She was upset, really upset. I can't say I blame her. Think about it.'

'All I can say is, it was lucky she didn't try it out on me.'

Steph was like that sometimes, a bit hard on the kids, and even, occasionally, a bit hard on me. Well, perhaps not hard, straight might be a better word. Or, perhaps, direct.

No messing, no dressing things up, no, to use a modern word, spinning.

Words spin in my head, like fishes in a pond, small coloured fishes, and you put out your hand to grasp one and it is gone, a flash of gold or green and it dives into the depths and your hand is left empty; they brush your fingers, teasing, gold and red, silver, blue and green, but you have not got the dexterity to catch one.

Stop.

Have a little sleep. Perhaps things will be better when you wake.

But why do you want to catch those words?

I don't remember. I just remember their importance in my life.

I never used to have this difficulty.

Never.

Perhaps . . .

Maybe . . .

Black.

*　*　*

I woke dizzy to find myself in my bed. I didn't know the time or the day.

Maybe, I thought, I had slept for days without waking.

The dizziness passed slowly.

It was daylight. A light rain tapped on the window, but strangely the sky was blue.

'So, you're awake.'

It was the nurse whose name I didn't know.

She was standing by the window.

'Twenty-four hours you've slept. We had to lift you into your bed and you're some weight, I can tell you that.'

She came across the room to me and put her hand on my forehead.

'Twenty-four hours. Well rested you should be after that. How do you feel?'

'Grand. I feel grand.'

'I'll go and tell Sister and don't you go slipping off on me while I'm out of the room.'

'I wouldn't dream of it.'

'That's the lad. I'll bring you some breakfast and a nice cup of tea. What do you fancy eating?'

I thought for a moment. I felt quite hungry.

'Scrambled egg.'

She smiled happily.

'That's good. Yes. Good.'

She was gone, leaving the door slightly open so that I could hear the bustle from the corridor. I liked that. I liked that connection with the world. I lay back and listened to the feet, the soft voices and the sound of rubber wheels on the polished floor.

*   *   *

They were all there in the house for dinner; Donough and Ciara and Brendan because when Stephanie had telephoned to invite Donough, he had said, 'And Brendan?' and she had answered, 'Of course,' and then regretted it for the rest of the afternoon.

She was making gravy, something she never did for herself, but complaints from the children forced her into it when they were around. Someone was playing old Beatles songs on the piano in the drawing room.

'All You Need Is Love' drifted into the kitchen.

'An unmusical bunch.' Brendan came in the door.

'They wouldn't agree with you.'

'Can I give you a hand? I think we won't have a piano in our house.'

'You could make some salad dressing if you like. You'll find everything there on the shelf. Garlic in the jar. You're probably wise, they've always been keen on the family sing-song. Individually they're OK, but put them together and . . .'

Dah da da da dah

'Pitiful.' He banged a knife down on a clove of garlic as he spoke the word. 'How was Henry today?'

She made a little face.

'I think he's going to be all right. He looks grim. His face is bruised and battered a bit, but that will mend. He was so pleased to see Ciara. He was always potty about her. She could always twist him round her little finger. It looks like she's going to go on doing that forever.'

'My father hated me.'

'I'm sure he didn't.'

'Despised might be a better word.'

'I'm sure he didn't despise you either.'

He laughed.

'Easy words to say.'

He was mashing the garlic in a small bowl as he spoke.

'I'm going to tell you something I haven't even told Donough.'

'Why? I don't think I want you to.'

He frowned into the bowl.

'Do you prefer balsamico or wine vinegar?'

She picked the bottle of balsamic vinegar from the shelf and put it in front of him without saying a word.

'Thanks I have to tell you.'

The piano and the voices rattled from the other room.

'We haven't time.'

'Yes, we've time all right. Steph ...'

She looked at his face, then nodded.

'All right.' She sat down at the table and put on what she thought was a listening face. He stirred at the mixture in the bowl.

'When I was eighteen ...' He paused for a moment and she wondered if he were going to continue or not. 'I tried to commit suicide.'

He banged the spoon on the side of the bowl. She put out a hand and took the spoon from his cold fingers. She nodded at him again.

'I haven't told Donough any of this. Maybe I never will. I had told my father, you know, about ... anyway I had told him. It was a Sunday, just after school was finished. Over and done with as far as I was concerned and ... well ... I thought I should. Mother had gone out and we were alone in the house and I just decided: this is the moment. He was reading the papers in his study and I just sort of slithered in and sat down. He looked up at me and smiled and held out a paper towards me. "Paper?" he said.'

'I thought you said he hated you.'

'Not then. Not before. No. I told him that I'd something to say to him and he pushed the papers off his knee onto the floor. I can remember it so well. It's like a film going round and round inside my head. I felt so brave and grown up and sensible – and honest. I thought freedom would come. You see I'd known forever and I had thought and thought about telling him and I really thought freedom would come. I looked forward to that. To be grown up and free. At that moment it seemed so simple.'

'I'm sure he loves you.'

'He smiled at me, encouraging me to tell him what was on my mind.'

'What did you say?'

' "Dad, I'm gay. I thought I should tell you." Just simple, like that. And he just smiled. "I shouldn't let it worry you," he said to me. "All that fumbling and groping that goes on at school. Lads of your age get confused. Give it six months. I remember it myself. It's part of growing up." He gave a little laugh then. "Boarding school was full of buggery. Masters at it too. It'll pass, son. Don't let it worry you." He smiled at me again and then as if he were a bit embarrassed by the conversation he began to scratch his nose. "This is for real, Dad," I said. "It's not a passing phase in my life. I'm gay. I know I'm gay. I've known for years that I'm gay. I'm telling you now because I don't want to be hiding things from you. Important things. I think you should know and Mother, of course, but it seemed easier—" "No. No." He stood up and held his hand out in front of him ... "No. Not your mother, please do not tell your mother ... No ... please ... No. No. No." And he left the room.'

There was a long pause.

Someone slammed a door and there was silence.

'What happened?' asked Steph. 'Then.'

'Nothing then. I just stood there feeling rather low and foolish. I couldn't quite work out what had happened or why. I I thought that he would understand. But . . .'

'But what?'

'He didn't. He was like you, a not-in-my-patch sort of person.'

'I'm not—' She stopped. 'Brendan. Get us both a glass of wine, would you? I'll have red. In that cupboard. Glasses are there too.'

She had a little spot on the inside of her cheek and she started to gnaw at it, chew it with her teeth. She broke the skin. It hurt. Damn.

There was a rumpus noise from the next room and then someone started to play the piano again. Brendan put a glass of red wine down beside her.

'Thanks. Did you have any more conversation about this? Or was that the end?'

'He didn't speak to me at all for a couple of days and then one evening when I was going to bed he came into my room. He walked across the room and opened the window. Then he fumbled in his pocket for cigarettes and a lighter. He lit up and stood there staring out of the window with smoke trickling out of his nose. I sat on the bed wondering what was coming.

' "About what you told me the other day. I have given it a lot of thought. I hope you have too."

' "Dad . . ."

' "I hope you have too."

' "I have worried . . ."

' "That's not what I want to hear. Damn it, Brendan, I do not want a — a son who is a homosexual. What do you say about that?"

' "It's not my fault, Dad."

' "I suppose you think it's mine, hey? What? Do you think it's mine?"

' "Of course not. It's no one's fault. Blame doesn't come into it. You know that as well as I do."

'He seemed to grow, like some huge ogre. The whole window became blacked out by his enormous size. I heard my mother call his name. There was a little pause and then she called again. He walked across the room and opened the door. He cleared the anger from his throat "I'll be with you in a moment, dear," he called to her. He closed the door again and turned back towards me, his son.

' "I have made enquiries, discreet enquiries I do have to say. We will go to England. They have ways there, they are more advanced in their methods of treatment. I have arranged for you to—"

' "No, Dad. I'm not going to England. I'm staying here. I'm going to Trinity. I'm going to be an architect, just as I've always wanted. I am not ill. I do not need treatment. I am a gay man. That's the long and the short of it."

' "And who may I ask is going to pay your fees, look after you, give you a roof over your head? Who?"

' "I hope you will pay my fees. For the rest I'll leave here if that's what you want . . ."

' "I most certainly do."

' ". . . and I'll get a job and pay for my own living."

' "And what will people say?"

' "I don't care what people say, for God's sake. My friends won't give a damn. I didn't think you would either and Mother—"

' "You're not to speak to your mother about this."

' "Don't be idiotic, of course I have to speak to Mother. I have to tell her the truth. She's got to know, just as you now know."

' "You'll break her heart."

' "Hearts mend. She'll probably be more understanding than you are." My father threw his cigarette in the direction of the window and missed by a few inches. I picked it up and stubbed it out on the windowsill and then dropped the butt down into the garden.

' "I don't know what's come over you at all," said my father, opening the door. "But I want you out of here fast." He left the room and stamped down the stairs.

'To get himself a stiff whiskey, I thought. Bastard. I thought that too.

'That's it . . . well no, it's not really, because I started to tell you another story, which I seem to have lost sight of. Perhaps now we have no time.'

'Your mother,' said Steph. 'What did she say? What was her reaction?'

'She cried. He got his drink and then went straight upstairs and told her. God alone knows what he said. How he put it. But she came into my room and cried. I put my arms around her and she cried and we just sat there in silence, except for her sobbing.

God, I felt such a brute. It was like I told her that I'd murdered someone. But as I sat there with her I knew in my heart that she'd get over it. That she'd love me enough to stay with me. I don't mean side by side, I mean in her heart and mind.'

Steph poured them each another glass of wine.

The dinner was going to be ruined, she thought, but what the hell.

The singers sang on.

Brendan took a sip from his glass.

'I left home and got a temporary job in an architect's office, emptying wastepaper baskets and that sort of thing, and I went to stay with a friend whose parents were away for the summer. I couldn't sleep. Each night I would lie down, exhausted and think, This night it'll be OK. And each night I would hear the clock down the road strike every bloody hour and I would hear her crying. Then when I got up in the morning I felt like I was sinking into the ground, the earth was sucking me down and down. I couldn't laugh or eat or feel anything except the weight that was on my back. My brave new world had collapsed on me, on top of me; I had no future, I had no present. My friend became very anxious about me and wanted me to go to the doctor.'

'I must say . . .'

'No. I told him, "I'll go in a day or two. I'm all right. I'm just tired, it's a hangover from doing my leaving." He believed me or anyway he didn't argue. I could see no life in front of me. I just felt this huge desire for death.'

He got up from his chair and walked in a tight little circle round the floor.

'I really wanted to extinguish myself. Now this is the bit I haven't told Donough, so please ...'

She shook her head; it might have meant anything.

'I had heard of all sorts of ways of doing away with yourself, but I really wanted the lazy man's way out, no swimming out to sea or hanging yourself on the back of the bathroom door with a dressing-gown cord.' He gave a little snort of laughter and sat down again. 'Pills? The gas oven seemed to me to be the best. Easy. Just stick your head in the oven and fall asleep. That appealed to me. I really needed to sleep, deep, dark sleep. So that night I went home. There were no lights on in the house. I let myself in the front door and went down the passage to the kitchen. Brandy, that was our dog, went mad when she saw me. She jumped and ran round in circles, she licked my face, my hands, she lay on her back and waved her legs, and she smiled such a huge smile at me. I had to calm her down, tickle her tummy, pull her ears, kiss her cold nose. Sssh, I kept saying to her, good girl, ssssh. She was a dear fat elderly spaniel. I had forgotten about her when I made my plan. When she had calmed down I put her out in the passage and she whined for a bit and scratched the door and then became quiet. I must say I was disconcerted by the session, I can remember uncertainty creeping into my head, but I quickly took Brandy's cushion from her basket and put it in the oven, then I turned on all the oven gas taps to full and lay down on the floor with my head on the cushion. I can still smell the dog smell. It was horrible. I buried my head in it, I shut my eyes. I thought if the dog smell ... the dog smell ... the dog smell and the next thing I knew was I was on the floor and my mother was slapping my face and shouting at me, "Bloody idiot, wake up. Up. Fool Brendan, wake up," and Brandy was snuffling in my ear and a wind was blowing in through the back door and I threw up all over the kitchen floor. Then she threw a jug of water over me. Cold water. I sat up. She threw a towel to me and I mopped at my head and neck.

' "What the hell did you do that for?"

'She started slapping my face again. And then she fell down onto the floor beside me and began to cry. I put my arms around her and we sat there for what seemed to be hours, with tears running down both our faces and the dog running from one side to the other, licking now my face, now hers. Finally she got to her feet.

' "Clear up that mess," she said, "and I'll make us a cup of tea." She stamped around for a while and I mopped up the mess and took the dog's cushion out of the oven and put it back in her basket. She seemed to think that everything was OK now, because she got into her bed, curled round for a moment or two and then went asleep. Mother made the tea in silence and then when she put the cup in front of me on the table, she threw her arms around me and held me to her.

' "We will never speak about this to anyone. Never. Never. Now, drink your tea and let's go to bed. You look like death warmed up." We both started to laugh and I didn't want to die any more. I have never wanted to die since that day. I want to live a long, long life.'

'Why did you decide to tell me this?'

'I suppose I want you to like me.'

'What happened to Brandy?'

'Long dead. Died happily in her bed. Sweet old life-saver that she was. I must get a puppy one day soon. Don't tell Donough that either. He might leave me.'

Stephanie laughed.

'He might and all.' She leant towards him, picked up his hand and kissed it. 'Our dinner is going to be ruined if we don't eat it soon and the children will rage at me.'

The door burst open and Ciara's head poked round it.

'We're starving. What are the pair of you up to anyway?'

'Sorting out the world, darling.'

'Can't we all sort it out and eat at the same time?'

Stephanie got up and went over to the cooker.

'My God,' she said. 'I've burnt the gravy.'

Somewhere Over the Rainbow, with Winter Coming Along

I got out of hospital on a November day. The wind was blowing the remains of the leaves off the trees. It was a cold wind, that brought tears to your eyes and made your spine shiver. From the north.

It was something I had forgotten about, but now remembered. You could smell the sea in its gusts. I took a deep breath and the cold air rushed deep down into my lungs.

I will live.

I had thought that as I stood outside the hospital.

I will live.

I had said my goodbyes and thank-yous, presents for the nurses and a bottle of gin for the sister. I don't know what she thought of that, but she thanked me politely. She stood now behind me at the door, the wind twisting her skirt this way and that.

'Go well. Mind yourself. Don't do anything I wouldn't do,' she called after me as I hobbled down the steps to the car. Jeremy was beside me, not wanting to take my arm and not wanting me to trip or fall. He opened the door of the car and helped me in. He threw a rug across my knees.

'What's that for, might I ask?'

God but I was becoming a cranky bastard.

He touched my shoulder.

'You may not have noticed but it's cold.'

'Thanks.'

'*De nada.*'

He shut the door and went round the car to the other side. Sister and two nurses waved from the steps. I waved back. They turned and scurried inside out of the wind. Jeremy got in and started the engine.

'Where to, sir?'

I was mildly startled; I had become so used to doing what I was told, following a regime, that I didn't think I would ever be able to make a decision for myself again. Even the decision for Jeremy to collect me had been made by him. He had overruled Stephanie's wish and indeed also Mother's, who had sent a message offering to send Mr Cook for me. I had put my hand to my head at this notion and muttered, 'No, no, no. Save me please from Mother for a day or two.'

'Ummm,' I said.

We drove slowly through the car park.

'I think we'll have a breath of sea air and then a good lunch. Put the roses back in your cheeks.'

'Will I ever be able to think for myself again?'

'Tomorrow.'

He gave me a dazzling smile and we turned onto the main road.

'Ta ra ra ta ra ra,' he sang tunelessly. He had always sung tunelessly, I remembered that.

'The beginning of your new life.'

'Singing is not one of your strong points.'

He laughed.

'We can't all be perfect.'

Something odd was happening to me.

'Look, do you mind driving slowly? My heart is beginning to thump. I didn't realise that ... that I'd be nervous. Just slowly please. I'm sorry.'

'I'm an idiot.' He slowed down. 'We'll change our plan. We'll go and look at the sea another time. I should have thought of that. We'll creep safely.'

'Thanks.' My hands were sweating and trembling. 'I feel such a fool. Will this go on forever? Will I never be able to drive again? Sit in a fucking car? Look.'

I held my shaking hands out towards him. He nodded and drew in to the side. I felt tears sliding down my cheeks.

'Oh God. Oh Jeremy. I can't do this. You'll have to take me back.'

He leant across me and locked my door. He put his arm round me and pulled me towards him.

My whole body was convulsed with shaking.

'Calm yourself. Calm. It's OK, pardner. It's all OK.' He rocked me like a mother rocks a child and after a few minutes I felt calmer.

I could hear Jeremy's voice talking. Burble, low, in my ear, his breath warm, in my ear, filling my head, warm soothing air and whispered words of comfort and love.

'You must take me back. I'm not ready yet.'

He pushed me away.

'Listen pardner. You've no choice . . . well, yes, I suppose you could walk home. How long do you think that would take? An hour at your debilitated speed. At least an hour. You might not make it even. The door is closed behind you now. There's probably someone else in your bed. Sister will have practised speaking other names. You cannot go back. So, I have to drive you. It won't take long. We'll go straight home and you'll be safe, I promise you that.'

There was silence between us.

Cars, buses, lorries, two men on motorbikes bucketed past us. No one even looked sideways at us.

He put a handkerchief into my hand.

'Wipe your face.'

I did. I blotted the sweat from my forehead and wiped my eyes. I handed it back to him.

'Keep it. We're going in a moment. Why don't you hold it in front of your eyes? Or would you rather get into the back?'

I shook my head. I clutched the handkerchief tightly between my fingers.

'No,' I said. 'You're right. Go on.'

He patted my shoulder, then ever so carefully put the car into gear.

I watched his hands on the steering wheel, long pale fingers, his knuckles creased and slightly swollen. I wondered if he suffered from arthritis. On his left wrist he wore a large gold watch which shifted slightly every time he moved his arm. He held the wheel lightly, touching rather than gripping. I closed my eyes. I pulled at the handkerchief, I knotted it and unknotted it.

'Music? Would you like some music?'

I shook my head. I could not have spoken, even if I'd wanted to.

'A jujube?'

I shook my head again.

'I'll shut up so and just concentrate.'

It seemed to take hours; stop, start, stop, start. At one moment he turned on the wipers. Swick, swick they went. Swick, swick and we splashed through puddles and the rain bucketed down on the roof.

Swick, swick.

'Are we nearly there?'

My voice sounded thick with panic.

'It's OK pardner, we won't be long.' He hummed a little discordant tune.

Swick, swick.

I cautiously opened my eyes and saw the grey sea on my left; little white horses broke the monotony of the colour. We bent round to the left.

'There's the Purty Kitchen. Would you like a bite there? They've good fish. First meal in freedom.' He slowed down.

'I just want to get home.'

He nodded and put on a little spurt of speed.

'Nearly there.'

I shut my eyes again.

We made it of course.

I sat in the car for a few minutes waiting for the shaking to stop. The garden around us looked weather-beaten and grey.

'It'll be better next time and we'll have you driving yourself in next to no time. You'll see.'

He helped me out of the car. I made it to the hall door without his help, but then was confronted by the stairs the other side of the small hall.

'We'll manage all right,' he said and almost carried me up and deposited me gently in the middle of the sitting-room floor.

I was home.

He was puffed.

'Wuh huh, wuh huh.'

I didn't recognise the flat.

It was nice; big windows, big balconies, view of the sea across rooftops, but it didn't seem to be my style at all. Expensive; a lot of velvet and puffed-up cushions, curtains looped back with silk ropes, fitted carpet. I felt uneasy. I felt very lost.

Jeremy looked anxiously at me.

'You seem surprised,' he said.

'I don't remember any of this. I must sit for a while and take it in.'

I sat down on what was, I must say, a very comfortable sofa and leant back among the cushions.

'I feel quite disorientated.'

'I'll make us a cup of tea.'

'That'd be good. Strong tea, not like the hospital hogwash.'

Jeremy left the room and I heard him rummaging in the

kitchen, turning on taps, opening the fridge, putting cups on a tray. I closed my eyes. I wished I were back in my hospital room listening to the corridor noises and the occasional snatches of the nurses' laughter. This seemed like another prison, better upholstered I had to say, but nonetheless a prison. He came back into the room and put a tray down on a table.

'You're exhausted.'

'I'll be all right. Don't worry. I thought I would recognise it. I'm a bit shaken by the fact that I don't. That and the drive . . .'

He put a hand on my shoulder.

'It'll all come back.'

'I hope to God.'

'I know, amigo.'

He ran his thumb up the back of my neck, delicate and delicious.

I shivered.

'Cold?' he asked.

I shook my head.

'I'm frightened.'

Warm fingers pressed into my flesh.

'There's nothing to be frightened of. I promise that. I will keep you safe.'

'You can't keep me safe from shadows.'

'I can keep you safe from everything. I know that. I love you. A great huge love. An umbrella of love I will hold over your head forever.'

'How daft you are. Umbrellas are no use when it comes to shadows. And of course love can die.'

'Mine won't.'

'How many times have you said that? Or I. Our capacity for love dies, let's put it like that. We become sensible as we get older.'

I shivered again, my whole body painfully racked by the shaking.

I waved a hand in the air.

'Bed.'

He nodded.

He hauled me to my feet and handed me my stick.

'I don't remember . . .'

Gently he took my arm and we moved towards my bedroom.

I recognised nothing.

The window was open and a soft breeze blew the curtains and there was a smell of the sea.

'I put on the blanket,' he said.

'Thanks.'

I sat on the edge of the bed, sweating and shaking, and he knelt down by me and pulled off the slippers that were all I had been able to fit on my feet, and then my socks. He was not as gentle as the nurses had been and I heard myself groan as he pulled down my trousers.

'Ssssh,' was a whisper in my ear. 'Ssssh now.'

My eyes closed. I felt him pulling off my jacket and then the warmth of my own bed embraced me.

I spent the day with my eyes closed; some of the time I was asleep, some of the time I was awake and could hear Jeremy's steps moving about the flat, occasionally the murmur of voices, the telephone bell, the sound of car horns and once the maroon summoning the lifeboat crew; my eyes remained closed and the breeze from the window touched my face and neck.

Poor buggers, I thought, out there in the sea, capsized into the sea, clutching at oars, spars, the keel, anything to keep afloat. Keep on top of that water, I muttered, hoping my voice would reach them wherever they were. Float. Help is at hand. Keep your head above water, in more senses than one. That was what I was going to have to do. Keep my head above the waters of the past, rushing me, pushing me, sucking at me, luring me, to some sort of benign madness.

Ha ha haha. Ha ha ha.

The laughter spouted inside me, burst up through my throat and out into the world. Was I drowning in laughter? My eyes jerked open. It was evening. Jeremy was pulling the heavy brocade curtains.

Ha ha ha. No.

'No what?' He turned to me.

Had I spoken the word?

I must have.

He paused in the curtain-pulling and I wondered for a moment how I came to have brocade bedroom curtains.

'No what?' he asked again.

'Don't pull the curtains. I like watching the sky change. I hate the dark.'

He pushed the curtains open again.

'Thank God you've woken up. I was afraid you might sleep that awful restless sleep . . .'

'I haven't been asleep. I just had my eyes closed.'

'You've been asleep for six hours, snorting and groaning, tossing and turning and then laughing. Fast asleep.'

'I was thinking.'

'You were sleeping.'

'I heard the maroon.'

'That was hours ago. Three idiot kids in a rowing boat. Only just outside the harbour. All safely rescued. Your daughter came round. Ciara, such magic hair she has. We tried to wake you, but it was impossible . . . so don't get cross.'

'Ciara?'

'She'll be back tomorrow and you'll be up and looking like a human being. Fret not. She brought you some flowers. They're in the sitting room.'

'Oh God, will I ever be well?'

'Of course. Now, how about you stagger to the bathroom and wash and then we can have a drink and dinner?'

'I don't think I can get up.'

'Of course you can. They wouldn't have let you out of hospital if they hadn't thought you could manage. Come on. I'll help you out of bed.' He pulled down the bedclothes and held out his arm for me to take.

We managed it. He handed me my stick and I limped across the floor.

'Good man yourself,' he said as I reached the bathroom door. It was a major achievement.

*   *   *

It was biting cold.

Stephanie ran the few steps between the car and the hall door and groped in her bag for the key. It swam somewhere down at the bottom always just escaping from her fingers. The wind from the north cut its way through her clothes.

'The air bites shrewdly; it is very cold.'

She could see a glimmer of light through the frosted glass in the window by the door and wondered whether to ring the bell.

'It is a nipping and an eager air.' She caught the key in her fingers.

'Gotcha.'

First signs of madness talking to yourself. She'd always been told that, but nothing had ever stopped her doing it; after all, she thought, look at Hamlet, talking to himself all the time, but of course there were those who thought he was mad.

'I've never seen him like that,' she said as she opened the door and stepped into the warn hall. She could hear the mumble of the television set, Ciara watching *Neighbours*, she thought to herself.

She switched on the hall light and called out.

'Yoo-hoo.'

She took off her coat and scarf and threw them on a chair. She walked down the passage to the kitchen. Might as well get the supper under way.

She turned on the radio. 'A ma...a...an of sorrows and acquainted with grief,' a gloomy voice was singing.

'Oh God,' she muttered and switched it off.

The telephone rang. She picked up the receiver.

'Hello.'

'Is that Stephanie?'

'Mmm.'

It was a whispering voice; she didn't like that, whispering voices boded ill. 'Look, it's Jeremy here.'

'Mmm. Where?'

'At home. He's locked himself in the bathroom and won't come out.'

'Who?'

'Henry. It's full of dangerous things, scissors, razors, pills . . .'

'I know what's in a bathroom.'

'What will I do?'

She thought.

'He'll come out in a while. Perhaps he's on the loo. Constipated. Something like that.'

'He's been in there an hour. He won't answer me when I speak to him. Honest to God, Steph, I'm a bit frightened. He might . . .'

'Rubbish. He's pulling your leg.'

'Please.'

'Please what?'

'Come.'

'And what good do you think I'll do?'

'Please, Steph.'

She sighed.

'I was just about to get the dinner.'

'Please.'

'I can assure you he'll come out.'

'No you can't. You've never known him like this.'

'He's not the self-damaging type. He's sulking about something.'

'Stephanie!'

'OK. OK. I'll be over. ASAP.'

'Bless you.'

Stupid bugger. She put down the phone and went to disturb Ciara who was watching *Neighbours*.

She put her head around the door.

'Ciara.'

'Umm. Oh hi, Mum.' She raised her hand in salute.

'Jeremy just called. He said your father's locked himself in the bathroom and won't come out.'

Ciara laughed.

'So?'

'So he wants me to go and try to persuade him or break the door down or something like that.'

'Why doesn't he just leave him there?'

'He's afraid he'll do something silly.'

'Really?'

'Really.'

Ciara switched off the set.

'I'll come too. It sounds more exciting than *Neighbours*.'

'I don't—'

'I'll come too. I bet he'll come out for me.'

*　*　*

He stopped his banging on the door and went away and I, poised on the edge of the bath, stared at the implements that I had found in the cupboard and put in a neat row on the shelf by the basin. One packet of razor blades and one safety razor, two nail scissors, one slightly curved, the other straight, one very old and blunt cutthroat razor, no strop, one beard scissors, one package of cotton buds for cleaning the ears and a tweezers: the thought of blood, all that blood gushing from me, spattering

127

the basin and dripping onto the black-and-white tiled floor, did not fill me with enthusiasm, so I pushed the weapons to one side and considered the rest: one bottle of bleach, for cleaning the lavatory, three boxes of painkillers, one bottle almost empty of sleeping pills and a pack of Immodium Plus. I picked up the bleach and put it down on the floor, beside the loo. Too much pain involved in that. I closed my eyes for a few moments and thought of the stuff rampaging its way down my throat, tearing off the soft pink skin and burning great holes in my guts. With my toe I pushed it further behind the loo. The desire for death was leaching away.

I could hear his voice muttering to someone on the telephone.

Soon the 7th Cavalry would come.

Did I or did I not wish to be rescued?

Would I rather take the first step myself?

I longed to be back in my bed.

I shifted onto the loo and put my head in my hands. I would wait and see what was going to happen.

I was so tired; never, never in the hospital had I been weighted down by such a weight of tiredness. I wanted to cry. I was crying, silently, my cheeks and the front of my throat were wet. I reached for a towel and held it over my face.

He knocked once more on the door.

'Henry.'

I didn't answer.

'Henry, please unlock the door.'

I held my breath in case he heard the sound of it. He rattled the handle.

'Please.'

Rain splattered on the window behind me, real winter rain with a touch of hail.

My head was aching.

I heard his footsteps moving from the door.

I mopped at my face and looked at the bottles of pills in a straight line on the shelf.

Eeny meeny miney mo, I thought; where do I begin?

Eeny meeny . . . I put out my hand for the sleeping pills. I unscrewed the childproof lid and shook some pills into my hand.

Stared.

Catch a— dear dear, word we're not allowed to use these days. By the toe. Even at the moment of our death. Not allowed.

Am I in love with easeful death?

I wish to be.

But how can I continue to live without my past?

The little tweakings of the veil will not content me. I want the curtain to rise, I want it all to be there for me, the ugly and the beautiful, the pains and pleasures. The grand opera of my life. My puny life.

I put the pills back into the bottle and screwed back on the childproof lid. Carefully I placed the bottle on the shelf beside the other bottles that I had taken from the cupboard.

The potential for easeful death was there in front of me. No blood, no pain, just a slipping away into darkness. Silence. Peace.

But then there might always be the possibility of the humiliation of the stomach pump.

I covered my face with the towel again.

There was another knock at the door and this time a different voice called me.

A timely knock, a timely voice, little above a whisper.

I felt my heart quicken; now that was good, I thought. It pounded a little, shoved the blood more quickly through my veins, pushed energy round my body. I threw the towel into the bath and as silently as I could I placed the bottles back in the cupboard, then those razors and scissors. I looked anxiously at my pale battered face in the glass over the basin. I frightened myself. Her voice went on whispering and cajoling on the other side of the door.

'Dad ... darling Dad ... open up ... please ... you're frightening us ... Mum is here ... we're sooo ... please ... you're going to get better ... your whole life is waiting for you ... please Dad ... Dad ... it's just us here, Mum, me and Jeremy ... and we need you to come out ... very soon you will be better ... honestly ...'

She rattled the knob. I smoothed at my hair. I cleared the phlegm from my throat. I hobbled to the door and unlocked it.

'Why,' I asked as I opened the door, 'can a man not have a crap in peace?'

'Dad,' was all she said.

I put my arms around her and hugged her, quite a painful thing to do.

I looked over her red hair at the other two standing side by side in the middle of the bedroom. Stephanie looked angry; Jeremy turned his head away as I caught his eye.

'What a fucking bastard you are,' said Steph. 'Come on, Ciara. Home.' Ciara clutched at my arm.

'Don't be beastly, Mum. We'll stay a while. We'll help him into bed.'

'No we bloody well won't. He can get himself into bed. I've had a horrid day, I'm tired, I have to cook the dinner, I need a drink and on top of all that, Mr Drama here decides he's going to frighten us all to death. I'm going home and you're coming with me. Now.' She hurled the last word at us all and turned towards the door.

Ciara let go of my arm.

'Mum ...'

'No.'

'Stephanie ...'

'No Jeremy, and the next time the bastard pulls a trick like this don't bother calling me. Come on, Ciara.'

'I have drink. I have food. Please stay. Come and sit down. Come and—'

'Mu ... um.'

'What?'

'We could stay for a little while. Fifteen minutes.'

Stephanie stood cogitating by the door. She suddenly relaxed and smiled.

'A very large gin and tonic would do me nicely. No, Ciara, we won't put him back to bed, he can bloody well come into the sitting room and watch me drink and make polite conversation.' She swept out and down the passage, followed by Jeremy.

Ciara touched my shoulder.

'I told her I'd get you out. I told her I was the only person would be able to get you out.'

I laughed.

'You're a brat.'

'But I did it, didn't I? I cajoled you. Didn't I, Dad?'

I kissed the top of her head.

'Were you really going to ... do yourself in? Was that what was in your mind? Dad. Dad. Dad.'

The third time she said the word it was in a low whisper. I just felt the warm breath of it pass my ear.

'Yes. But for God's sake don't tell anyone. Anyone.'

'You won't do it when we go? You won't even think of doing it ever again? Promise me.'

'Ciara.' Stephanie's voice called from the other room.

'Promise.'

'Ciara.'

'Coming. Promise.'

She looked like she might attack me viciously.

I held my hands up in the air.

'I give up. I will not die. I will not resort to taking my own life. I promise.'

'I love you so much Dad, I couldn't live without you. I thought I should tell you that.'

She put her hand gently under my elbow and pulled me towards the door and I thought as I went with her how lucky I was to have such a child. I felt quite choked by my love for her, and foolish for my ridiculous notion that I might kill myself.

They walked across the floor to meet me as we came into the room and led me to a chair, neither too low nor too high, just the chair for someone unable to cope with the normal things of life, a chair filled with cushions and a rug thrown casually across the back in case a draught touched me and made me melancholy.

Ciara remained beside me, leaning on the chair, a beautiful guard, and the other two stared their own private stares at me, Steph still angry, but smiling, Jeremy upset and anxious.

'I'll have a drink.' I settled myself back into the cushions. 'A whiskey, I think, please. No water, just a couple of rocks. How nice of you both to come. I'm sorry I wasn't quite ready. You're looking very well, Steph, a little pale but well.'

'Just shut the fuck up,' she said. 'I'm sure you shouldn't drink neat whiskey. Not just after that little exhibition.'

'Pay her no heed,' I said to Jeremy. 'She's a matron manqué.'

He smiled mournfully at me.

'Well,' he said, handing her a gin and tonic. 'I did wonder . . .'

'Don't. I wonder enough for all of us. If you're all going to fuss and bother about me, I may as well go back into the hospital.'

He dropped two ice cubes into a glass and poured some whiskey in on top. He walked across the room towards me.

'Are you living here with Dad?' asked Ciara.

'Yes.'

He put the glass into my hand and touched my shoulder.

'Forever.'

Stephanie clunked her glass down onto a table.

'Are you . . . ?'

'Ciara!'

'Are you . . . you know? Are you . . . ?'

'Ciara!'

I took a slug of whiskey and rattled it round in my mouth for a few moments before swallowing it.

'What do you want me to say?' Jeremy asked Ciara.

'I want you to tell me the truth. Are you and Dad . . . ?'

'Ciara. It's time we went.'

'How old are you?' asked Jeremy.

'Sixteen.'

'Ciara, I'm going. So if you want to walk home . . .'

She moved towards the door.

'. . . in the rain . . .'

'Yes,' said Jeremy. 'We are.'

'Ooooh!'

'I think you're old enough to know the truth.'

Steph had reached the door; she opened it and stepped outside.

'Ciara!'

Ciara bent and kissed me on the top of my head.

'Love you, Dad. Coming, Mum.' She turned from me and put her arms round Jeremy's neck. 'I think I love you too. Thank you for telling me. Mum and Dad would have waited until I was thirty or forty or never. Now we all know where we are. See you soon. Remember your promise.'

She was gone.

'That's a one,' said Jeremy.

'I'm exhausted.'

'I'm not surprised.'

'Should that have happened? Should you have said that to her?'

'Of course.'

'I'm not sure it's true. I don't remember. I keep searching and searching in my brain. I . . .'

'They all have to know sometime.'

'You sounded so certain. I don't feel that certainty. I'm sorry ...'

'I am certain.'

There was a long pause. I felt the heavy hand of tiredness pushing me down into the chair.

'I have to sleep. It's been such a day. I really need to sleep.'

'Finish your drink and I'll help you to bed.'

I shook my heavy head.

'I'll drink it in bed. I have to ...'

I began to push myself up out of the chair. He was beside me, hauling on my good arm; together we got me to my feet and leaning on him I shuffled to the bedroom.

'I don't need help. I must be able to undress myself.'

He stood staring at me.

'You mustn't be angry.' He took my shirt from me and shook it. He hung it on the back of a chair. 'You do remember what you said, "Lord what fools these mortals be" and—'

'Motley's the only wear. What cute little mixers of quotations we were. And of course it isn't true. Away with the motley.'

'Everything will be all right.'

'Time will tell. Maybe it will. Tomorrow, we'll talk.'

He bent down and pulled off my slippers and my socks and then gently raised my legs onto the bed; he pulled the bed-clothes up over me and then I heard her voice calling to me.

'Henry, Henry.'

From beyond the grave the calling voice that I had heard before and I said, 'No,' and fell asleep.

Even in my own bed I had troubled sleep.

Her voice, alluring, luring, calling and then his voice, Jeremy, melting, mixing into hers and they both called me.

Henry.

God how I hated that name.

Always had.

What, I wondered, possessed Tash to call us such terrible names?

I woke up for a little while and the moon shone through the window and the room was filled with silver light and I willed myself to remain awake, but my eyes refused to stay open and the voices and the fingers of sleep pulled me ... and her hair was long and red ... no, that was Ciara and she called too, not Henry, but Daddy, softly; I could barely hear her voice and then hands wound me round and round in a long skein of red hair and I couldn't move and her face hovered over me, or was it his face, and I couldn't move. I was their prisoner tied with Ciara's hair.

'Help,' I shouted. 'Please, help me.'

And no one came.

* * *

'I read somewhere that one man in five is gay.'

Ciara was beating eggs as she spoke. Her mother stood by the cooker drinking a glass of red wine; Brunello di Montalcino, too good for moments like this, she had thought as she opened the bottle, but she needed its comfort. She let the wine rest on her tongue for a long moment, filling her head with its fragrance, and then let it trickle slowly down her throat.

'Nonsense,' she said finally.

'I've read it.'

'You shouldn't believe everything you read.'

'And we've got two of them in our family.'

'Ciara . . .'

'There's no point in arguing, Mum.'

'It's maybe one in twenty. No need to beat those eggs to death.'

Ciara put the bowl on the table.

'But what is odd, what I don't understand, is that Dad didn't leave you for a man, he left you for a man's sister. Don't you find that odd?'

Her mother picked up the bowl and poured the eggs into a frying pan. She looked at them for a moment and then gave the pan a vicious shake.

'I don't want to have this conversation.'

'You're going to have to. Another thing I don't understand is why grown-ups, adults never want to talk about things that their children want to talk about.'

'You couldn't possibly understand . . .'

'I want to. I really want to.'

Stephanie poked at the eggs with a knife, ran the blade round the edge of the pan, shook the whole lot again.

'Put some knives and forks on the table, would you? When I was sixteen I knew nothing. I played hockey, I went to the pictures. My pals and I, well we speculated, we read, but we knew nothing. I think it's better like that.'

'That was then. This is now. Anyway if you read you must have known something – about the dangers in store for you, that sort of stuff. I can't believe the dangers have changed. Have they?'

Stephanie turned off the gas under the pan.

'Get me some plates and please, please lay the table.'

Ciara made a face, but did as she had been told.

They were silent. Steph poured herself another glass of wine.

They remained silent as Stephanie dolloped some omelette onto a plate and handed it to her daughter.

'What's this?'

'Don't be tiresome. You know quite well what it is.'

'A broken to pieces omelette.'

'Just eat it.'

'May I have a drop of wine?'

'No.'

'Why are you being so mean?'

'I'm tired. I want to go to bed. I don't want to sit round for hours talking unsettling rubbish with you.'

'It's not unsettling rubbish.'

'As far as I'm concerned it is. Tomorrow I may feel differently. Tomorrow I may not feel tired. Tomorrow . . . I would love this day to be over.'

Ciara got up and put her arms around her mother.

'I'm sorry,' she said. 'Truly sorry. You didn't know?'

Stephanie shook her head.

'I didn't know.'

'Not even suspected?'

Stephanie didn't speak. She shoved some food into her mouth and chewed.

'Mum . . .'

'Eat your supper and leave me in peace. I promise you we'll talk about this tomorrow or – sometime.'

'Sometime schumtime.'

'Don't push me too far, Ciara.' Her voice was weary.

Ciara nodded abruptly and left the room. Stephanie listened to her running footsteps on the stairs and then poured herself another glass of wine.

* * *

On the morning of my third day out of hospital, the sun shone in a clear blue sky, the rooves of the houses across the park glittered with frost, sparks seemed to rise from the earth, rushing into the sky.

No one called my name, no one sighed in my ear. The silver clock on the table by my bed showed me eight thirty. I could hear him moving quietly in another room, a slight cough, the clink of china, water ran. I pushed back the clothes and manoeuvred myself out of bed. I stretched my useable arm; that felt good. I felt good – well, comparatively. I limped to the window and stared out into the sunshine and the sparking frost. I felt giddy for a moment and leant my head on the cold window glass.

There are things I have to ask, I thought. I feel so ragged inside my head.

I heard movement behind me.

'When was it that we met?'

'You're up?'

'Yes. I feel better today.'

'I've brought you a cup of tea. I expected to find you lying there angrily with your eyes shut.'

"'Oh my God, is that the way I've been?'

'Yup.'

'Never no more. I promise you that.'

'I'll believe it when I see it.'

He put the cup down on the table by the bed.

'Fourteenth of December last year. You barely spoke to me. You were in a rage about something.'

I laughed.

'You stood by the window staring out at the darkness and hardly said one word. Not exactly welcoming. Charlotte had insisted that I should come and we'd all go out for dinner together. We'd really make each other's acquaintance, learn to love each other. You remember the way she used to go on like that.'

'No. I remember nothing about her at all. Well, except our meeting – that is . . .'

'Whatever was going on that evening she was nervous as a cat and chattered like a mad thing, watching you all the time. She never took her eyes off you. I don't think you heard a word she said. I thought you were pretty grim, I must say. I took her out to dinner, you refused to come and she sang your praises all the time. She said you'd had an unsettling letter from one of your children. Something like that. Drink your tea before it gets cold.'

'Were you at our wedding?'

He shook his head.

'Why not?'

'I was in Australia.' His voice sounded evasive. 'I was working for an architect, a guy who had studied with me. He had gone out there and set up and invited me to go and work with him. We were, well, together for several years. Together. You understand?'

'Of course I understand. What happened?'

'It got a bit ropy. He was not made for monogamy and I couldn't bear the way it had all become, so ...I came home. About as far away as I could get. That was when we met. Well, we had actually met before, but only for a second. I don't think you even noticed me.'

'No ...I'm sorry. When?'

'You only noticed ...her.'

I picked up the cup and took a sip of tea. Furious anger was gathering inside me.

'Just bloody tell me. The truth. That is what I want now. Need. I need the truth.'

His face went red and then white; he put up his hand as if to protect it from me, either my fists or my eyes, it was difficult to tell.

'It was some party or other. I was home for a couple of weeks and we both went wearing the same clothes, black velvet jackets and trousers. It was a throwback to our childhood. We really used to fool people then. Just a bit of fun. I wore make-up and she didn't wear any.' He laughed. 'So you see. It was fun.'

'Yes. I can see it might have been.'

I was the one who had been fooled.

A brush of a touch on my face.

I looked at his hands; they were small, long-fingered, strong. He wore a gold signet on his little finger.

'You fooled me.'

'We fooled everyone that night. It was such fun. We laughed all the way home in the cab. I think the driver thought we were pissed out of our minds, but it was just happiness. Pure and simple.'

'It was perhaps a foolish thing to do.'

I got up and walked over to the window, carefully carrying my teacup. I sipped and stared out at a black and white cat that was cleaning itself in the middle of the grass.

'Are you angry?'

'Yes. No. I am very confused. I feel I have been duped. That's not a good way to feel. I hate that. What exactly was it supposed to achieve? Who was I supposed to fall in love with? Was it all done so that you two could have a good laugh in the cab on the way home? Yes, perhaps I am angry.'

The cat got up and stretched itself, leg by leg, and then sat down again.

'Very angry.'

'I can understand that.'

'Thank you so much.'

Jeremy sighed.

'It's such a weight off my back. I have to say that. To have spoken about this. To have told you. You see she double-crossed me too. She waited until I had gone back to Sydney and then she phoned you. She wooed you . . . this I do promise you was not part of our silly game. She didn't tell me about any of this. Not a word. I just got this phone call saying she was getting married to guess who. I didn't believe her. I thought she was pulling my leg. You looked so settled at that party, so glued to matrimony. I touched your face with my hand and whispered to myself, I am touching the face of a married man who I know I could love. She had no such scruples. She went for you, I went back to Oz.'

The cat stood up once more and lashed its tail from side to side for a moment or two and then walked off with feline dignity. I am the cat that walks by itself; it disappeared round the corner of the house. Tash hadn't been a wonderful mother, but she had read us that story. I remember her voice and the youth of her, sitting on my bed and pointing at each word with a long finger and the slight smell of turpentine that came from her hands as she moved them. I am the cat that walks by itself and all places are alike to me. She had worn a blue dress. I remembered that too.

'Where have you gone?'

Jeremy's voice.

'Sorry.'

'I just wondered where you had gone. You disappeared.'

'I was looking at a cat.'

'Minky. He lives next door. He catches birds. Actually I think he's a she. A hunter-gatherer she. That's the way it is with cats. The males sit at home on cushions.'

I laughed.

He touched my shoulder.

'That's better. I like to hear you laugh. It makes me feel less wretched.'

His hand was light on my shoulder; two of his fingers stroked my neck; pleasurable, I thought to myself.

Oh yes.

He sighed, a quiet sigh.

'This of course may not work. You know what I mean. This. Us. It . . .'

'It may not.'

'You may or may not remember how we felt. That joy may not return. Never. Enormous joy. I can only describe it as that.'

I put up my hand and held his fingers.

'I'll try,' I said. 'I really will.'

His fingers pressed the side of my throat, where the little pulse beats. Perhaps trying wasn't going to be too difficult.

'I'd better get dressed,' I said.

*   *   *

Snow came.

It lay along the branches and the railings in front of the houses; it lay on the hedges and on the wires that held inside themselves the telephone noises and the electricity; it lay on the rooves and bonnets of cars, not all that much, just a dusting of white, a smattering.

'I think,' said Steph, 'I'll invite everyone for Christmas.'

She stood looking out of the window at the smattered garden, with her second cup of morning tea clutched in her two hands. It was Saturday; no school fuss, no work fuss, in fact, if you played it right, no fuss at all.

Ciara was eating bacon and eggs at the kitchen table.

'The snow is early this year. What do you think?'

There was a robin on the path below the window, standing quite still, like a tiny statue she thought.

'I must put out some bread for the birds. Poor things, how they must hate this weather. It's strange you never see dead birds lying around. I wonder what happens to them? Have you lost your tongue?'

'I'm eating.'

'You can talk and eat. I asked you a question.'

'Everyone. You said everyone?'

'I did.'

She held a hand out in front of her and ticked off the fingers.

'Dad. Jeremy. Donough. Brendan.'

'Yes, all.'

'And Tash?'

'Of course. It wouldn't be Christmas without Tash.'

'George?'

'Don't be silly, darling. He's in Toronto.'

'You could ask him, couldn't you?'

Stepanie took a large mouthful of tea and let it slowly trickle down her throat. She thought about George.

Dear old George.

The robin hopped, then stood for a moment, its head twisting from side to side.

'The north wind doth blow and we shall have snow,' said Steph. 'And what will the robin do then, poor thing?'

'Robins are well able to look after themselves. The toast is cold.'

Her mother drank some more tea.

'I like George. He sort of holds things together.'

She put a lump of butter on the cold toast and mashed it around with her knife.

'I might go to Toronto to university. Now there's a thought. I could live with George. I must find out about the English department. If he comes for Christmas I might pick his brains. I know there are lots of people who look on Canada as a great big yawn, but I like the sound of it. What do you think? Mum? Hey. Ma?'

The robin hopped onto the grass.

How cold its poor little feet must be.

'Mother. Stephanie. Hey.'

'What? Sorry, did you ask me something?'

'Holy God.'

Stephanie left the window and went over to the table. She sat down and took a piece of toast.

'This toast is cold.'

'I said.'

'I was thinking about George. Perhaps I'll give him a ring. Should I ask your father first?'

'Nah. Whose house is it anyway. Don't breathe a word, not even to Tash. Big Christmas surprise.' She giggled. 'We could dress him up as Santa Claus. That'd be fun. I'd say we might need a bit of fun. Go and ring him now.'

'Don't be an ass, it's about four o'clock in the morning. I'm going to feed the birds.' She broke up the toast into tiny pieces and left the kitchen.

Ciara smeared a thick layer of marmalade over the butter.

She thought about love. Dangerous stuff, she thought, paths of mystery along which everyone seemed to have to stumble at some stage in their life.

The toast wasn't too bad.

Couldn't it be avoided? If you kept your head there must be a straight road from the cradle to the grave. Find it. No cutting corners, like Dorothy and her three companions and the dog. What was the dog's name? She searched for a moment or two.

Toto?

Probably.

Somewhere over the rainbow, way up high.

She only discovered who she loved after she seemed to have lost them all.

Apart from Toto, but loving Toto didn't count.

Dogs!

I will keep away from all that stuff.

The chunks in the marmalade were very dark and very bitter. She smiled; like love, she thought, and then what do I know about it anyway. I'm a child still, Mother thinks that and Dad too, I am his red-haired star. I thought for so long that I hated him; I thought I would never speak to him again as long as I lived; I thought my being had been corrupted by my hatred of him. But that's OK now. I love being his red-haired star. I don't care if he is gay. I think that's cool; here and now. Yes. Here and now. Where's the harm? Grown-ups are so daft; they keep piling on these rules, what you can do, what you can be, what you can say. Alarming. The thought of becoming one of them, joining that enormous club, full of idiotic rules. I will always be around for you, lovely Ciara, he said that to me so many times and then he wasn't. He forgot me. Love took him and shook him and shook all of us out of his brain and he left us. She was beautiful. I saw them once in Grafton Street. I dodged into a shop when I saw them coming and peered out to get a good look at her. The one. How had she managed it? I wondered that as I peered out of the door at them. She was beautiful, but not half as beautiful as I was going to be. I thought that. She will become a pale shadow beside me, I thought, and I sauntered out into the street and right past them. Ciara, he said, and I turned my head away. I felt happy and miserable at the same time. I cried all the way home in the bus. I hate him. That's what I said almost aloud and the tears streamed down my face. He used to take me to the zoo. I didn't like the zoo. Sunday afternoons and tea. One of the waitresses said to me one day, 'I remember your daddy when he was a little boy, roundabout your age he must have been. He used to come here with his granny, and his brother too. The pair of them had the poor lady worn out. Dashing here and there, everywhere, the pair of them was, one as bad as the other.' I loved him then, loved the thought of his small-boy naughtiness. He used to run his hands through my hair, tickling the back of my neck. He used to blow noisy and tickly kisses on the back of my neck. I am probably too old for him to do that any more, but I really miss it.

There's a land that I dreamed of once in a lullaby.

Yes.

And now I am in a muddle once more because I love him and I don't know whether this upsets Mum or not. I really don't want to upset her. She doesn't need upsetting. Dad has upset her more than enough. It's odd really, him leaving her for that woman, and he isn't that way at all. There are things I'd like to talk to him about, but you can't really. Things that are too private and those bloody grown-up rules apply. And then you say one day I'll wish upon a star. One day I'll ask him. One day he will tell me what I want to know. One day he'll blow a kiss on the back of my neck. One day we will be a happy family again, but fate or God or unsuspected accidents happen. Motor cars crash, people fall downstairs, they drown, here one minute and gone the next leaving their unfinished business behind.

What, anyway, is a happy family?

Do I know one happy family?

Do I know one happy person?

I was happy when I was little. I know that.

I remember being happy, even at the horrible zoo with Dad. At the seaside, the back of my hand tasted of salt and little sparkles of sand seemed to be embedded in my arms; wrist to elbow, as if I were made of gold, and I sat on the edge of the sea and put salty stones in my mouth. I swallowed three. I was afraid that I would die; I never told anyone until now. I was sure I would die and be lifted to heaven by gentle hands.

And wake up when the clouds are far behind me.

I didn't know then that happiness was an uncertainty. It is this growing knowledge that turns children into grown-ups. I don't want to go there, but I know I must. Yes. I want to have a long long life and plenty of memories. I want to have children and grandchildren and great-grandchildren. I don't ever want to die. My views about gentle hands lifting me to heaven have changed.

Somewhere over the rainbow, skies are blue.

*　*　*

Dear Dad. I would like to spend time with you. We have missed so much of each other and strangely enough I don't mind you being with a bloke, it was the woman I really objected to. Now, at last there is truth. Truth counts. Truth does count. Who was it said that? In what book have I read that? Anyway, and to end, I love you.

She looked at the words for a long time before reaching for an envelope and writing the address on it. She folded the paper neatly in three and pushed it into the envelope.

'Mum,' she yelled.

'What?'

'Stamp.'

Her mother appeared in the door, glass of wine in hand.

'Supper's ready.'

'Have you a stamp?'

Steph frowned for a moment.

'A stamp.' She said the word as if she had never used it before.

'You know, you lick it and put it on an envelope.'

'Cheeky. Are you being cheeky?'

'I don't think so. I just want a stamp.'

Her mother took a drink of wine.

'I'm not very good on stamps. Try the right-hand top little drawer of my desk. Then come and have supper.'

There were no stamps.

She carried the letter in and put it down beside her mother on the table.

'No stamps.'

'Hmmph.' Steph looked down at the envelope. 'What on earth are you writing to him for? No. Don't tell me. I wish we were more orderly. You could try and be orderly, I'm too old now.'

'It's just a note. Probably a bit silly.'

Her mother patted her shoulder.

'He'll be delighted.'

'You think?'

'Yes, darling. I know.'

'You see I once sent him a terrible letter, so this is to counterbalance that.'

Her mother sighed.

'I'll post it tomorrow. I'll leave a note for myself; post Ciara's letter. I will be orderly. I really will.' She began to laugh. 'Think how mad the world would be if everyone were like Tash. Everyone just living life exactly as they wanted to. No order.'

'I think it would be rather splendid. No school, no silly grown-up rules and regulations, people dancing in the streets and painting wonderful pictures. It sounds like heaven to me.'

'Let's eat before our supper gets cold.'

'Rules, rules,' said Ciara.

* * *

'Christmas is coming and the geese are getting fat,
Please put a penny in the old man's hat.
If you haven't got a penny, a halfpenny will do.
If you haven't got a halfpenny, God bless you.'

I brushed my hair and sang, if you could call my croaking singing.

George and I used to caper and sing in front of our parents and their friends at a party they always gave just before Christmas every year. Their friends sipped their drinks and smiled benignly at us and threw sixpences into our hats, sometimes even shillings. Once someone had put a ten-shilling note in, but Tash had made us give it back.

'Christmas is coming and the . . .'

'You're a cheery little soul today.' Jeremy stuck his head round the bathroom door. 'Dressed and all.'

'. . . geese are getting fat.'

'Are you feeling better? I haven't heard you singing before.'

'Well not exactly better, but getting there. I'll be out in a tick.'

I could hobble now with great care and a lot of time, my shoulder no longer hurt and my face looked good once more.

'Please put a penny in the old man's hat.'

I patted some aftershave on my neck.

'If you haven't got a penny ... You know each scrap that comes into my mind, bad or good, brings ease with it. Strange but true. What are we going to do about Christmas?' I arrived at the table and lowered myself into a chair. Jeremy had piled every hard chair with big, soft cushions; my comfort seemed paramount to him. 'Bless you, bless you,' I muttered. He poured me some coffee.

'Steph rang after you were asleep last night, about Christmas. There's pain au chocolat, if you like, or just toast.'

'You're going to have to stop spoiling me like this, you know. Each day I can do more for myself. Toast, please. What did Steph have to say?'

I put quite a lot of butter on the toast. I love butter; maybe I will become a fat old man.

'She wondered if we would like to go to her for Christmas dinner. The children will be there and Tash and whatsis-name, you know, Donough's bloke. She says he's a terrific cook and she and he are going to lock everyone else out of the kitchen.'

'It could be hell on earth.'

'Well ... hardly.'

'You don't know Tash. I'm sure she will have something up her jolly little sleeve. She'll die or something.'

Jeremy laughed.

'After we've eaten I hope. I said I'd ring her. What do you think?'

'I suppose we'd better go. The kids and all. It's been such an age since I spent Christmas with them. The rest can go hang.'

'No presents, she said.'

'Rot and rubbish. We'll go on an expedition in the car and buy lots of extravagant stuff. The excitement will be so great that I won't be frightened at all.'

'OK.'

'Is that all right with you?'

'Of course.'

'Sure?'

'Certain.'

'And loads of memories of loads of Christmases will come back to me and I will be cured. My whole life will be freed up once more. A miracle. Mind you . . .'

'Mind you what?'

'I just wonder if Steph is up to something.'

'I wouldn't think so. I honestly don't think she wants you back. Anyway, even if she did all you have to say is no. No thank you. Unless . . . unless, of course . . .'

'We have to talk.'

Jeremy looked alarmed.

'No need for upset. You must tell me the truth.'

'Truth. I have never told you lies.'

'About you and me and Charlotte. You know I can't remember. You will have to tell me. I must know. I have to face the children and Steph and I must know what happened. If you can unravel that mess for me . . .'

Jeremy poured himself a cup of coffee and went over to the window. He stared out at the grey day.

'It doesn't have to be now, not this minute. Sometime soon though. I feel at such a disadvantage.'

'I would rather that you remembered yourself. I might not tell the whole truth. Anyway where's the rush?'

He sipped at his coffee.

I loved his every movement; the way his head stooped forward and the stretch of the muscles in his neck. The flop of his hair.

'As far as I'm concerned there's rush.'

He nodded. He continued to stare at the greyness. He was silent. I crunched my toast. I was nervous; I had trouble in swallowing, so I washed the toast down with a belt of coffee.

'The truth will set me free?' I tossed the words in his direction. 'So they say.'

'Once upon a time . . .' he started.

'I want truth, not fairy tales.'

He turned from the window and faced me.

Once upon a time I was whole and happy, I thought; no broken bones, no mind misted with forgetfulness, my children loved me. I was normal.

What is that? Normal?

He was speaking. I crunched some more toast. I listened.

'Once upon a time, and in spite of your objection I will begin like that, there were twins, like peas in a pod, everyone said about them, except for the fact that one was a boy and the other a girl. Their mother and father played silly games with the children, they used to dress them in each other's clothes and encourage the little dears to confuse people, grown-ups and children alike. They thought it was charming. They thought it was witty. They were people who thought that charm and wit were the be-all and the end-all.'

He took another big gulp of coffee.

'They themselves called the children Sebastian and Viola, when the mood took them. Which I do have to say was quite often. Sometimes I was Sebastian and sometimes Charlotte was. You learnt to answer to whatever name was called, but that was private. To the world at large we were always Jeremy and Charlotte. I preferred Sebastian; Jeremy is quite a creepy name, don't you think? "Darling S", my mother used to call me. Darling S. Yes.

'We loved it. We loved fooling people and not getting punished for it. The older we got the more we loved it. We weren't bad, just badly brought up. We enjoyed pulling the wool over people's eyes. Sometimes we even managed to fool our parents. That really annoyed them, but they had taught us to do it, so they couldn't be too angry with us. They were killed driving too fast on their way to the races at the Curragh. Poor buggers. In their prime they were. Here one minute and gone the next. Perhaps that was what was in her mind when she ...' He paused and I wondered whether to take his hand or not. I decided not.

'She was the ring leader; I'm not making excuses for myself, I enjoyed very much becoming Viola, but I preferred to do it among friends, rather than follow her into more dangerous waters. The softening of the voice gave me pleasure, and the occasional fluttering of the hands – you remember how her hands used to flutter from time to time, like the wings of a small bird?'

'No. I don't.'

He held out a hand towards me and it fluttered; he touched the side of my face, his fingers vibrato, displacing the air. I said nothing; I was anxious to listen rather than to talk.

'She liked lads and I do have to say that sometimes we shared them, she might filch mine or I hers. That was all good fun, nothing serious, we were young and handsome in our own ways. We were jokers, gamesters, out for a lot of laughing. We laughed and flittered and fooled people all the way through college and then I went to Australia. Neither of us was heartbroken, we each managed to live equably without the other. We never wrote long moaning letters; short, brisk phone calls were more our style. Hey sister, ho brother. All well with you? See you. Soon. Soon. Soon. That sort of stuff. No confidences, no tittle-tattle tales of conquests or broken hearts. I worked hard, I lived for several years with the man who was my boss, as I told you. I had grown up, I wanted a calm life, but he didn't. I decided to go home for a week or two to see what would happen. She was in a mad mood. Oh God, and so pleased to see me and I thought it would be good to be bad again for a while. So we went to that party and we both met you.'

He moved away from me and took an agitated turn around the room.

'Oh God,' he repeated.

His hands splayed out in front of him, then prayed, fingers intertwined.

'Oh God.'

I kept my words imprisoned in my throat.

'She saw you first. I do have to give her that. Finders keepers. I was talking to someone, I don't remember who, some girl or other, being the boyish me. Charlotte came up to me and put her hand on my shoulder and whispered in my ear, "Look behind you and a little to your right," and she was gone through the crowd. The girl I was talking to looked startled. It's OK, I said to her, we're twins. Then, I turned and saw you. Profile, you were looking solemn, through the smoke and breath of that party, your head was bowed towards someone. You looked up and seemed to catch my eye and I felt my face getting red. I was blushing, something I had no recollection of ever having done before.'

He pulled a chair out from the table and sat down. He smiled nervously towards me. I nodded.

'Well, blushing, like a schoolboy or not, I moved towards you and put my hand on your arm. Your attention was all on me now.

' "I've come to say goodbye."

'Now, why the hell did I say that? I don't know. I was going away, back to Australia, I suppose, and I was never going to see you again. Something like that went through my head. I whispered the words. Perhaps I didn't want you to hear them. Or perhaps my voice might have given me away.'

'You have to say hello first,' I said.

'You remember?'

'You were wearing pale pink nail polish.'

'I touched your face.'

'You said hello.'

'I moved away, towards the door. I had to go. Back to Australia.'

'Stephanie called me, and I called after you, wait. Who are you?'

'I didn't hear. I promise you I didn't hear. Otherwise . . .'

'It's a fairy tale.'

'All true.'

'Lac des Cygnes.'

'Oh la la! Have some more coffee.'

He nodded, but didn't move.

'Odile won.'

'Odile is dead.'

I put out my hand and took his.

'Odette is left with a pretty damaged prince.'

He laughed and pressed my fingers.

'Temporarily.'

'We'll hope.'

'Odette is very full of hope.'

'Have some coffee.'

Slowly he let my fingers go and reached for the coffee pot. I watched him pour for a moment or two.

'But you're going to have to tell me the rest, you know. I have no recollection.'

He poured milk into his coffee, stirred it and watched it whirl.

'You may not believe me.'

'Why would you lie?'

He laughed and took a large, long drink of coffee.

'For fun,' he said. 'This all started out for fun, you know.'

'Get on with it.'

I took some more toast and put lots more butter on it.

'I went back to Sydney. I didn't say a word to Charlotte about you before I left. This is just a flash in the pan I said to myself, the least said the better. Sydney is a great city. We might go there sometime, you and I. Not just to Sydney, but we might travel for months, see the whole country, before somehow someone civilises it. It is monstrously exciting. Sorry, wrong story. My partner, lover, whatever you like to call him, was not blissfully happy to see me back, so we split, amicably I have to say. I continued to work with him and I found myself a wonderful flat, all glass windows and on the edge of the bay. Cost a fucking fortune, but I was earning a fucking fortune too and I had no one to spend it on but myself. I almost bought a Nolan, God, I wish now I had, but then it seemed foolish. One of his Antarctic ones, do you know them?'

I shook my head. I have never been a Nolan fan.

'Wonderful. Land where no person has been. Clean and amazingly dangerous, and bright.

'Anyway I didn't. I mightn't have come back if I had, Australia's so bright too. I loved that. All the world's brightness spread out there before me. But I dreamt of you, when I dreamt. You were always there, unsettling me, smiling, a come-on smile and then she rang me and told me . . .'

He got up from the table and walked over to the window.

'Yup,' he said. 'She rang and told me.'

I waited.

'It's not really my story any longer. It's hers and yours.'

'I can't remember. You must believe me, I've tried and tried. These black holes in my head are really painful.'

'Nothing?'

'How many times do I have to tell you? Absolutely nothing. Other things seep back, but not her, not our life together. The children hated me; I remember that. I have these little visions of hate . . . I had letters from her, Ciara. Maybe I imagined them, maybe I tore them up and threw them away, but I remember the pain of reading them; I have no letters from her. I have nothing from her, only this, the state I'm in. I don't even recollect this flat, just the books and an odd picture. No Sidney Nolans.'

He ran a finger down the window pane; for a moment my stomach churned.

'She had discovered who you were before we left the party and your address and telephone number. She was a real operator. She told me with such triumph in the car on the way home. Henry, she laughed as she spoke your name. Such a foolish, old-fashioned name. Why would anyone call their son Henry? Answer me that? Leave him be, Charlotte, I said to her; apart from anything else, he's well married. We'll see, and she leant over and pressed my hand, gave it a little tickle actually with one of her long nails, we'll see. I swear to you I knew no more about her plans than just that. I went back to Australia the next day and I knew nothing until she phoned me and told me that she was getting married. I must say I was pretty surprised; I had never thought of her as a marrying person. She loved men, but not forever, not really even for very long. Until . . .'

He squeaked his finger down the window pane again.

'Don't do that,' I said angrily. 'It makes me feel sick.'

He moved away from the window and stuck both his hands in his trousers pockets.

'She never used to get the time right. So it was about three thirty in the morning when she rang. I was fast asleep. Oh God, I thought as I woke up, someone's dead. Who? Who? And I said who as I lifted the phone and I heard her laugh coming all the way across the air waves. She sounded as if she was in the room with me.

' "Only me, darling."

' "It's three thirty in the morning."

' "I am so, so sorry. But I've news that can't wait."

' "OK. Spit it out and let me get back to sleep."

' "I'm getting married."

' "Oh."

' "To Harry."

' "Harry?"

Yes darling. You remember the lovely man you picked up for me at the—"

' "But he's married."

' "Not for long, except of course to me. He's living with me now. Well, he's at work at the moment. I thought you'd like to know."

' "It could have waited until tomorrow."

' "Not as far as I'm concerned. I am so utterly happy, blissfully and utterly . . . we are both so—"

' "Tomorrow. I will listen to your ecstasy tomorrow."

'I put the receiver down. I couldn't sleep. I felt I would never sleep again. I felt like a bloody pimp, disgusted with myself. Some awful mistake had been made. The word kept beating in my head. Over and over. Mistake. Mistake. There must be some awful mistake.'

His voice disappeared into a whimper.

Outside the window tiny flecks of snow blew in circles, down, down towards the city. Swirled down, settled and then melted. The sky was like a huge grey sheet, pulled tight over us. My head was hurting.

He was silent.

Something throbbed just above my right eye. Was it a memory, I wondered, trying to beat its way out of the darkness?

He had begun to talk again but his words went nowhere; they wandered round the room, not finding their way into my head.

I tried to find the sound of her voice.

Was it her voice I had heard in my head when I was in the hospital? Or was it his? Or some stranger to me?

We are so blissfully and utterly . . .

How could you forget such happiness?

Was every emotion so forgettable?

What about my marriage to Stephanie, had that also its utterly and blissfully happy moments?

Why had I left her?

Had I made her miserably unhappy, or was she glad to see the back of me?

What was a long marriage like?

'You're not listening.'

He had crossed the room and was standing directly in front of me.

'I am trying to remember.'

'You'd do better to listen to what I'm saying.'

'It means nothing. It's just a story. It could be about anyone, any time.'

He squatted down beside my chair and took my hand in his.

'It is about you and me . . . and her. I promise you that. It seems to me that if you and I are to have any chance together you must remember and believe. Otherwise we have no hope. We'll just end up a pair of lonely old buggers.'

He squeezed my fingers. He ran a nail across my knuckles.

'Did you ring her back?'

He lifted my hand to his mouth and put his lips against my fingers.

'No.'

The word vibrated up to my shoulder.

Nnnnnoo.

I felt it inside me.

'She rang again about a week later. This time it was daytime. She had at least learnt that bit of sense. It must have been a Saturday or Sunday, because I was there. She got me. She said it all over again, even the bit about being blissfully and utterly . . . you know. And I said, you told me all that before, and I put down the receiver. I couldn't bear to hear her triumphant voice for another second, so I just plonked the bloody receiver down and went for a walk. She always wanted everything in life to go her way, she always wanted what I had and she didn't mind cheating to get it. All our lives she had always won and always I had hung around and smiled. Weak-kneed. Yes, yes, yes, but this seemed too much to bear and I howled as I walked. I'm surprised someone didn't come along and lock me up.'

His head was on my knee and I stroked his soft hair. I

remembered suddenly the feel of that hair, only it must have been her hair, soft and thick; my fingers had loved it.

I thought though of George and how different he had been; he had always backed slowly away from things that he had known I wanted.

I remembered.

The memories were leaking like water finding its way through holes and cracks in its container. George's face smiling at me; George howling, his fists stuffed into his eye sockets and a stinging slap from Tash across the back of my legs. 'Leave him alone, don't bully him. He's only a baby. Don't tease him.'

A dark winter morning, wind causing the window behind me to rattle and the curtains to sway gently in the draught. The door opened; I kept my attention fixed on the typescript in front of me. He coughed twice, softly, as if he didn't want to disturb me. I pushed the papers to one side.

'Yes, George? I'm really very busy. Can it wait an hour or two?'

He shut the door behind him.

'Sorry, bro.'

He took two steps towards me.

'I just wanted a word or two, but if you're busy . . .'

I sighed. I patted the papers into a neat pile.

'What is it? Sit down.'

We stared at each other across the table. I waved at the pile of papers.

'This is rubbish. Strictly for the birds. Sub chick lit, but I bet someone else will publish it. Do sit down, George, you're making me nervous.' He sat down. I smiled ferociously at him. 'Well? Get on with it.'

'I'm going to Canada.'

'You've made up your mind at last?'

'Well yes . . . umm yes.'

He looked past me and out through the window. In spite of the stormy weather someone was cutting grass with an old-fashioned lawn mower which ticked along past the window and then turned and ticked back again.

'It's to do with . . .'

His fisted hands lay on the table in front of him; I wondered if he were thinking of hitting me, or howling.

'Umm . . . Stephanie. Yes.'

'Stephanie?'

He nodded. He cleared his throat. He closed his eyes.

'George.'

He opened his eyes. They were large and blue, like Tash's.

'I love her . . . I'm sort of crazy about her and . . .'

'And what?'

'I just thought I ought to ask you . . . I wondered. Well, that's all.'

It hadn't occurred to me until that moment that I might marry Stephanie; that there might be a glorious safety in marrying her.

Safety?

Why, I wondered, had that word come into my head?

'I just wondered if you'd told her . . . you know.'

'I haven't the foggiest idea what you're talking about.'

'Robert O' Carroll.'

He unclenched his hands and laid them flat on the table. His face was red, and I felt mine going red too.

'I don't know what you're talking about.'

'Yes. You do.' *We were both silent for a long time; the lawn mower ticked outside and somewhere a dog barked and I thought of Robert and I remembered the humiliation and the pain that had filled my whole being for weeks and the fear and Tash's laughter and the way she had tousled my hair as she laughed and said, 'We all have secrets, Henry.'*

'That was nothing. Absolutely nothing. How did you know about it anyway?'

'I had eyes and ears. I was alive. I used to listen at doors, you know. I've always found it sensible to know what's going on around.'

'It was childish nonsense. Your eyes and ears should have told you that. Nothing happened. We were best friends, that's all.'

'His mother rang Tash. Did you know that? Tash told Father, they thought it was funny. I heard them laughing.'

'I don't believe you.'

'It doesn't matter whether you do or not. I just think you should tell Steph.'

'Why? What business is it of hers or yours for that matter? Or anyone's?'

'It might . . . she might . . .'

Fury rose inside me.

'Bloody damn fool. You imagine she'd look at you. You imagine she'd up sticks and go to Canada with you. What a total idiot you are.'

He fisted his hands again.

'I'm just thinking of her,' he muttered.

'Liar.'

'She ought to know. She ought to see the picture. The whole . . .'

I pulled the pile of papers towards me and began to read once more.

He stood up.

'Bro.'

'Just shut the fuck up and let me get on with my work.'

'Steph . . .'

'Out.'

He left the room and I sat and listened to his footsteps crossing the landing. He opened his bedroom door and went in. He closed the door behind him. I tiptoed downstairs to the telephone and rang Steph.

Later that evening we got engaged. Having remembered all that, I wonder now, why?

Why?

Tash raised her eyebrows at me, as much as to say why, when we arrived home after dinner and told her the news.

'How perfectly lovely, darlings. Lovely, lovely. Nothing quite like a wedding to put a little cheer into people.' She paused and thought for a moment or two. 'Funerals are quite cheering too. Some of the best parties I've been to have been funerals. George is going to Canada, did you know that?' She turned to Stephanie with a beaming smile. 'Not of course that there's any connection.'

'No, I didn't know that. I didn't think he'd made his mind up yet.'

'He's such a silly boy. I expect he'll come back quite soon. What do you think, Henry?'

'I haven't the foggiest idea. It's up to him really.'

'Hmmm.' She closed her eyes and waved a hand at us. 'Great news, darlings. Lovely day ahead. Lovely life ahead. You'd better go and tell your father.'

That was my recollection.

I sat quite still at the breakfast table and thought about George.

And outside the snow twirled and danced and the dark grey clouds seemed to sink lower and lower, pressing against the roof tops.

✳   ✳   ✳

'George.'

'Hello.'

'Is that you, George?'

'Hello. Who is this?'

'Stephanie.'

'How amazing. Hello, Steph. Is anything wrong?'

'No. Everything's fine. How are you, dear George?'

'Well. A bit startled to hear your voice, but well. It's snowing.'

'It is here too. Amazing.'

'It's great to hear your voice.'

'We all wondered would you come for Christmas. I know it's short notice, but we'd love it if you could. It's been so terribly long. Dear George, please think seriously about it.'

There was a long transatlantic silence.

'Are you still there?'

'Yes.'

'We thought we'd have a real family Christmas. All of us. All odds and sods. Tash thinks it's a great idea. You could stay here. There's Donough's room. He's moved out, you know. So you wouldn't have to stay with Tash.'

'Under no circumstances.'

'And Henry and Jeremy. They're coming. They're together. Did you know that?'

George started to laugh.

'What's funny?'

'Nothing. I'm just happy to be asked. I'll get my tickets this afternoon. So Henry's come out.' He laughed again. 'About bloody time. How splendidly dysfunctional you've all become.'

She felt a stir of anger inside.

'You knew?'

'Well . . . no. Of course not. I had the odd suspicion. Listen, back to the subject. I'll come for about ten days. If you can put me up for so long.'

'George . . .'

'I'll stay till just after New Year. Is that OK?'

'Yes, but George . . .'

'So long. Must fly. I'm so looking forward to seeing you all. Kiss, kiss.'

And he was gone. She put the phone down and lay back in her chair.

'Am I the world's biggest eejit?' she asked herself aloud.

* * *

Ciara was painting her toenails, a very bright frosted pink, when Stephanie went into the kitchen. She sat on a chair with her foot propped on the edge of the table. Her face was filled with alarming concentration.

'What on earth are you doing that for?' asked her mother. 'And darling, not on the table. Please.'

Ciara paid no attention to her mother; she leant forward frowning slightly at her smallest right-foot toe, then dabbed at it with the little brush.

'No one will see them,' said Stephanie. 'At this time of year. I mean to say that's summer stuff. Sandals and all that.'

'I will see them. I will know how pretty they are under those tights and boots and things. When I take off those outdoor things I will see them, bare and pretty. All sparkly.'

'Well whatever, take that foot off the table. Now.'

Ciara moved her foot. She stretched her legs out and smiled with satisfaction at her toes.

'I rang George. He's coming. Isn't that great? I must ring—'

'George.' She twiddled her toes and smiled. 'Oh, Uncle George. That is great. We can get to know each other. I can prepare him for my running away from home trip.'

'You are to behave yourself. There are going to be enough problems without you thinking up one too.'

Ciara stood up and looked down at her feet.

'Don't you think they're lovely, my twinkle toes? And Henry's coming and Jeremy? Like you said, you've invited everyone? I don't cause trouble. Everyone loves me so they do. All those people who are coming, anyway.'

'Hmmm. Don't put your feet back on the table. Lay it for supper instead. I'll ring Tash.'

She went over to the kitchen phone and dialled Tash's number. Tash's voice was blurry when she answered.

'Yes, yes, yes. Who is it?'

'Stephanie.'

'Yes, yes, yes, darling, how nice of you to ring.'

'Are you all right?'

'Of course I'm all right Why wouldn't I be all right? Why would I not?'

'I've just been talking to George.'

'George who?'

'Your George. My George. Our George.'

'Oh, George. He's not here, is he?'

'He's in Toronto.'

Tash began to mumble incomprehensible words to herself, little stuttering words, that made no sense to Stephanie.

Th-th-thun, they went, wee thggg.

'Tash! Tash. Do you want me to come round?'

'No. Do not come round. I am perfectly. Perfectly. Do not under any circumstances come round. Why were you talking to George? Dear old George.'

'He's coming for Christmas.'

'All that way?'

'For ten days.'

'I must go and make his bed.'

'No, darling, no need. He's going to stay here.'

'Nonsense. He's my George. Dear old George. I'll make his bed.'

'It's all arranged, darling. He's going to stay here. He can spend each day with you, but he's sleeping here. That's what he wants to do. That'll be the easiest for all of us.' There was a long silence and then Stephanie became aware of the sound of sobbing.

'Tash. Tash.'

No reply.

Shuffling footsteps and then silence.

'Tash.' She shouted the name.

Silence.

Stephanie put down the receiver and stood with her head in her hands.

'What's up, Mum?'

'Tash is being very peculiar.'

'She's always pretty peculiar.'

'I wonder if I should go round.'

'It's snowing.'

'I could get a taxi. She's left the telephone off the hook. She just walked away. Slip, slop, I heard her feet going. I think she's gone to make George's bed.'

Ciara laughed.

'She's probably had a drop too much.'

'Or she's ill.'

'Have you ever known her to be ill?'

Stephanie thought for a moment.

'Not in public. I don't know what she gets up to behind her own closed doors.'

'Leave her so, to her privacy.'

'You're probably right. We'll have supper. Oh God, what madness have I let myself in for? I'm exhausted by Christmas already.'

'We'll all row in, Mum. It'll be fine. It will actually be wonderful.' She did a little circular dance around the kitchen.

'Will you be normal when you grow up? Please be normal. One normal person in the family would make me so happy.'

'What's normal?'

'I thought I knew. But I was wrong. All the way.'

Ciara stopped her little dance and went over to her mother. She put her arms around her, hugged her.

'What is normal?' she whispered again in her mother's ear.

'You must be. For me.' She pushed herself away from her daughter and went over to the cooker. Saucepans were bubbling and clicking. 'You must get married and have babies and live in a neat house. That's normal. That's what I want you to do.'

'A prison sentence, you make it sound like.'

'Nonsense,' said her mother. She stuck a fork into a potato. 'Five minutes. Please lay the table.'

'Nobody lives like that any more and anyway I think I'd like to be an actress.'

She took some knives and forks from the drawer and plonked them down on the table, then went to fetch plates and glasses.

'You know, that's the first time I've said that to anyone, but it's been a dream in my head for quite a long time. I see myself filling a theatre with my beautiful voice.' She threw her arms wide and embraced the room. 'I will learn how to do that. I will play all the great parts and love them all, even Lady Macbeth, I will really love them all. Mum, I can hardly wait. Isn't that a dream. Shouldn't we all have dreams, not just decide to be normal?'

'Yes, darling, of course we should. I think we should open a bottle of wine and drink to each one's dreams.'

*   *   *

My second drive in the car I sat with my eyes shut, and Jeremy manoeuvred us carefully through the traffic to the Dundrum shopping centre.

'All human buying is here,' he said as he parked in the gigantic garage. 'No need for you to distress your poor broken body. Lifts, escalators, coffee shops and Christmas decorations.' He hauled me out of the car and handed me my stick. 'We'll start at the top and work down.' Everything sparkled and shone.

'I don't think I have ever been here before. It doesn't seem like the sort of place I would have shopped in. It rings no bells in my head.'

'You spent too long locked in your little rat-run, doing the things your parents did and Steph and her parents and then along came Charlotte and the new Ireland.'

'Well I can't remember any of it. Thank God.'

Jeremy took my hand and kissed it.

Everything sparkled and shone and somewhere some people were singing carols.

'The holly and the ivy, now both are full well grown, of all the trees that are in the wood . . .'

Shining high children's voices threw the words up into the dome above them.

'. . . the holly bears the crown.'

People pushed and shoved.

'Oh the rising of the sun and the running of the deer': mixed voices now.

Jeremy tucked his arm under mine.

'Are you OK?'

'. . . The playing of the merry organ . . .'

'This is insane.'

'. . . Sweet singing in the choir.'

'It's the new Ireland. I'll protect you. How about a coffee before we plunge into the shops?'

'Yes, yes.'

We pushed and shoved our way across the current of the people and went into a small coffee shop.

'Sit,' he ordered and pushed me down at a table by the window.

'. . . The holly bears a blossom as white as . . .'

The sound of the singing was no longer as loud; in a window across the way I could just see, through the pushing and shoving crowds, the heads of two reindeer bowing and rising, bowing and rising. Silver and gold baubles hung from the ceiling, swaying gently in the breeze created by the passing crowd; everything swayed, bowing and rising, like the reindeer. I felt myself doing the same thing, holding gently on to the edge of the table to prevent myself from falling on to the floor. I felt seasick.

'There.' He put two cappuccinos on the table and sat down. 'You look dolorous.'

I laughed.

'I'll recover. I like that word. Dolorous. It's the new Ireland. I feel no connection with it. I think I'll stay at home in future. Never go out again.'

'Don't be such an ass.'

'I might become a writer. I've read so many bad books, I feel sure I could do much better than most of the writers who send us stuff. Stuff. Damn stuff. I'll just sit at home and write, me and a computer.'

'And me.'

I laughed again.

'That goes without saying, old dear, and of course visitations from my red-haired Ciara.'

I scrambled in my pockets for a pen and a notebook. 'Let's make lists,' I said. 'We can't go on a real shopping spree without a list.'

We set to, to the sound of the singers.

> 'Oh the rising of the sun
> And the running of the deer,
> The playing of the merry organ,
> Sweet singing in the choir.'

I went straight to bed when we got back from our shopping. I toed off my shoes and lay on top of the bedclothes and I drifted into dreams to the distant sound of Jeremy taking things from plastic bags, unwrapping packages, murmuring to himself as he did so and humming little snatches of songs; songs I couldn't recognise.

She and Stephanie stood on each side of my bed. Steph mute and faded-looking, the other, though dressed in black, was like the shopping centre, effervescent and joyful.

I heard myself sigh.

I got up from the bed; I could move with ease, no broken bones or even memories of stiffness and bruising.

She held out a hand towards me, and whispered something that I couldn't hear. I glanced towards Steph and saw tears like huge Christmas baubles rolling down her forlorn cheeks. I put both my hands in my pockets, determined to touch neither woman.

The walls, pictures, the door, the long window and curtains disappeared, strip by strip rolling up into some dark heaven above until all that was left was me, in the darkness, and the two women, each in her own spotlight. I wanted to run, but my legs were imprisoned on the black floor. Superglue, I thought to myself, only superglue can hold me tight like this. My fingers in my pockets even seemed glued together; my lips wouldn't open; all I could do was move my head looking towards one woman and then the other. She whispered something else; she was enticing me, she held now in her hand a glittering dagger, its handle encrusted with jewels, diamonds, emeralds, rubies. I knew what was in her mind, that I should come to her. Use the dagger, come to me, she was whispering. Come to me. Come to me. I couldn't speak. I wrestled with my lips; I needed to shout for help.

No.

The word was only in my head.

She smiled at my discomfiture.

And her smile was also an enticement.

I turned my head towards Stephanie; her figure was fading, the edges becoming soft, misty.

Help me.

These words also were in my head.

I don't want to die. I don't want to go to her.

Help me.

I felt her hand on my arm.

No.

'I thought a cup of tea would be good.'

Jeremy was beside the bed, bending over me, touching my arm.

My lips burst open.

'No.'

'What do you mean, no?'

'I didn't mean that. Thanks. I was having a terrible nightmare. She . . .'

He put the teacup on the table by the bed and sat down beside me. He stroked my head gently.

'There, dear heart. There. You're awake now. You're with me. You're safe. She can't hurt you.'

'Oh God, will this go on forever?'

'Of course not. We were out for too long. You were exhausted.'

The door, the window and its curtains, the walls were all back in place. Snow drifted down outside from a grey sky.

He picked up the cup and handed it to me; my hand was trembling.

'Drink,' he said.

'She wants me to die.'

'She's gone. You know that. A dream is only a dream. Drink some tea. It will all drain away as time goes on. She's gone. I will protect you. Go on, drink some tea.'

I took a sip from my cup; it was delicious, smoky and very hot. I could feel it scalding me right from the back of my throat right down to the tubes and skeins that wound around in my stomach.

'That's good,' I said. I took another sip and enjoyed the pain.

He stood watching me; his face drooped with sadness, or perhaps he too had been exhausted by our shopping.

'Come and sit beside me,' I said. 'You look tired.' He sat down on the bed. 'Share my tea . . .' I pushed the cup towards him.

'No thanks. I've already had some.'

'When are you going back to work? I'm OK now. I don't need looking after all the time. I'm actually thinking of starting to work again. I can do a lot of stuff at home and Claire can come in a couple of days a week and deal with post and all that sort of stuff. My head needs an occupation, it really does. After Christmas I will start. Oh God, I feel so happy just having said that to someone.'

I took another long drink, a mighty swig; in fact I drained the cup and put it down in the saucer with a clatter.

'Yes. Energetic mind work. I can hardly wait.'

'I love you so much.' He took my hand. His eyes were enlarged with tears.

'I don't know. I can't say that to you, because I don't know. I can't remember. I'll have to learn all over again. I cannot remember what I felt when I loved someone. Not just you. Anyone. The knowledge of that feeling, that ... emotion has disappeared. How do you know? How do you fucking know? When the memory of that is gone, is it gone forever?'

He stroked my fingers.

'It will come back.'

His voice was low and sweet, like a woman's; like hers had been? I wondered.

'But you do remember that night on Sandymount Strand? That came back to you.'

'Light-heartedness.'

'Perhaps that's what love is. Perhaps that's all you have to remember.'

'I don't think it's as easy as that.'

He put his arm around my shoulder and pulled me close to him; we sat, my forehead against his cheek, for a long time in silence and he stroked my fingers and the snow outside became quite fierce, each flake fighting the wind on its way down to the earth, and I felt safe and drifted into a peaceful sleep.

Perhaps, I thought, perhaps.

* * *

Henry's flat was the top half of a fine Victorian house near the top of Glenageary Road, and the wind swept down the hill blowing snowflakes and crisp packets with it on its journey. Ciara, wrapped and bundled like a parcel, pushed her way up the hill. The wind pulled at her, buffeted her, tweaked her hair out from under her woolly cap, and the passing cars splashed her with dirty water. She spoke aloud to herself and whistled and sang little snatches of song, to keep her face from freezing. No one else was walking but far in the distance she could hear carol singers. 'O come all ye faithful,' they sang, backed by someone playing a guitar, 'joyful and triumphant.' She sang along for a moment or two and then she couldn't hear them any longer so she stopped.

'I'm trundling,' she said, and the wind hit her a smack in the mouth. The whole world seemed to be trundling, past houses lit by Christmas trees, some outside, their lights swaying in the wind, some glowing inside, safe from the punching wind. She turned into the driveway of the house and all was white and silent. There were lights on in their flat.

She went round to the side of the house where their door was and rang the bell. She stood on the steps and looked back at the bay; the snow was easing off and she could see right across the black water to Howth where lights twinkled like little stars, and the beam from the lighthouse swept and swept through the darkness.

She rang the bell again and Jeremy's voice answered the intercom.

'Yes.' He sounded weary.

'It's Ciara ... You know, Ciara. Is Daddy ... ?'

'Come up.'

The door buzzed and she pushed it open; she shook herself like a dog does after swimming, then she stepped into the warm hall and as she walked up the stairs she unwrapped herself and dropped her wet scarves and coat on the floor at the top of the stairs. Jeremy stood watching her.

'Wouldn't you like to hang them up?'

'They're OK.'

'Your dad's in bed.'

'Is he all right? I just thought I'd like to see him.'

'He's perfectly all right and he's very glad to see you.'

Henry stood in the doorway of his bedroom, fully dressed but without shoes, and his hair was uncombed.

'I must be up when my daughter calls to see me.'

He held out his arms towards her and she moved slowly towards him. They embraced and he held her close to him.

'Your face is freezing.'

'It's freezing out and wet and I feel all red and horrible.'

'Tea? Coffee?' suggested Jeremy.

'Perhaps a glass of wine?' suggested her father.

Ciara giggled.

'Now that would be most acceptable. That would warm the cockles of my heart.' She giggled again.

Her father pushed her towards a chair.

'Sit. Sit, my child.'

'Daddy . . .'

'Sit.'

She sat down on the velvet sofa and he sat beside her and took her hand.

'Red or white?' asked Jeremy.

'Red, please. Daddy, I hope you don't mind me dropping in like this.'

'I'm delighted, my darling.'

'You seem much better.'

'I am. I can walk quite well without my sticks now.'

'Not for long. Will you have some wine too?' Jeremy was opening a bottle.

'Oh yes, I think so. The cockles of my heart need warming too.'

'You really are coming for Christmas? You won't change your minds at the last moment? You won't chicken out? Will you?'

Henry laughed and squeezed her fingers.

'Of course we're coming. We wouldn't miss it for the world. We've been to that hell hole in Dundrum and bought presents for everyone.'

Jeremy handed her a glass of wine.

'It nearly killed us both.'

'We don't want presents.'

'Well you're bloody well getting them and you'd better like them.'

'Uncle George is coming.'

'Oh my God, more presents to buy. I haven't given George a present for twenty-five years.'

'I bet Mummy has, on your behalf.'

'Probably.'

'Will you stay and have supper?' Jeremy asked suddenly. 'Then I could run you home in the car.'

'No thanks. Mummy will be expecting me. Another time though. That would be lovely.' She took a drink from her glass.

'Lovely wine.' She muttered the words almost to herself.

'Nothing but the best here,' said her father.

She pinged a finger against her wine glass.

'There's just one thing I'd like to ask you.'

'Fire ahead.'

She went a little red and looked about ten years old.

Jeremy moved unobtrusively towards the kitchen door.

'I must just . . . ah, the dinner . . .'

'No. Please don't go. I'd like you to be here.'

He stopped in his tracks and looked towards Henry. Henry nodded at him.

'Stay. By all means.'

She began to gabble.

'I don't want anyone to think that this has anything to do with Mummy. It hasn't. I love Mummy. I love her to bits. Honestly. So, you mustn't . . . No, I couldn't bear it if you were to think anything . . .' Her voice filled with tears. She swallowed and no one spoke for a moment or two and then she continued. 'I just wondered if you'd let me come and just . . . live with you for a while. After Christmas, like next term. Here. Just for a while. I am very house-trained. I promise. I'd be no bother. Honest to God.'

Henry looked startled; he pulled at his nose, rubbed the corner of his eye, didn't speak. Jeremy stared into his glass of wine.

'Please Dad,' she said.

He didn't look her in the eye.

'I'd have to discuss this with your mother. It's not that I wouldn't . . . please don't get the wrong idea. It's just, well, I'd have to talk to your mother about it. Let's leave it till after Christmas. I'll speak to her when all that's over.'

Jeremy coughed gently.

'And of course Jeremy. I couldn't come to any decision without Jeremy. After all . . .'

'Of course.' She poured the remains of the drink down her throat and stood up. 'I understand. I really do. I'll go. I'd just like you to know . . . I've missed you, you know. Those years. I've regarded myself as a half-orphan. That may sound silly to you and now I feel as if I must . . . must make up all that loving time. I . . . have missed you. I don't know if I love you or you love me and I really need to . . .'

The tears in her voice came back.

'Darling . . .'

She shook her head and swallowed again.

'You're probably saying child's stuff to yourself. That's what Mum thinks anyway. Always.'

'Of course I'm not.'

'A child feels things too. All children feel and it's probably made worse for them because they don't have the experience or wisdom, whatever you like to call it, to help them understand. It's kept from them. Their loving parents keep it from them.'

She was really crying now. Her father struggled to his feet and went to her. He put his arms around her and held her tightly against him.

'Baby, darling baby.' He murmured the words into her hair. 'We'll work something out. We really will. I'll come round tomorrow and talk to Steph. Here.' He handed her a handkerchief. 'Wipe your eyes. You look a sight. Jeremy will drive you home. No arguments. It'll only take a few minutes. Mop up, baby.'

'It's OK. I can . . .'

'Jeremy will drive you home. No argufying.'

She smiled at the word he had always used. She touched his shoulder.

'You'll come tomorrow. You promise.'

'I'll ring her and we'll arrange something. Tomorrow morning, I'll ring.'

She nodded. She turned towards the door.

'*A demain*,' she said as she left.

Jeremy sighed and followed her.

❉   ❉   ❉

I was on my third glass of wine when Jeremy returned; as usual I was struggling to remember not just little flashes of memory, but stretches, something I could get my teeth into, gnaw on, like a dog. A wonderful giant bone was what I needed.

'Nice girl,' he said, throwing the car keys onto the table by the window.

I nodded.

'Where does the red hair come from?'

I thought hard, but no ideas came to me.

'I can't remember. Must have been somewhere in Stephanie's family. My mother's hair was black.'

I would brush it for her, long and very black, sparking as the brush ran through it. Not red, nor auburn, nor gipsy carrot. Black as midnight. She would sit with her eyes closed, humming softly as I brushed.

'She had a silver hairbrush.'

'Who?'

'Oh, my mother. I used to brush her hair in the evenings before I went to bed. True. Yes. I wonder what I did with her brush, she gave it to me when I got married. Steph had her own, so it was put away somewhere.'

'Was there a bird on it? With huge outstretched wings.'

'Yes.'

'You must have given it to Charlotte. It's on the dressing table in my bedroom. Beautiful.'

'Yes.'

I was suddenly angry with myself for having given my mother's brush to this unremembered woman.

'I'll get it for you.'

'Don't bother.'

'No bother.'

'Another time will do.

'What are we going to do?' I asked him.

'About Ciara?'

'Mmmm.'

'Hard to say. I'm sure that Stephanie will have a point of view.'

'She will. But you, would you mind if she were to come here? Live here with us for a while.'

He looked me straight in the eyes.

'It's up to you. She's your child. You know that. I can always move out. I can go back to my old flat, or else into your room. It's for you to decide. Whichever you prefer.'

His voice was light, careless. I felt my face and neck getting red.

'Of course she can't come and live here. It's a crazy idea. She must stay with her mother. She can come for the odd weekend. She ought to realise that she can't muck up people's lives like this.'

I poured myself another glass of wine.

Silly child, I thought. Dear, silly child. My. Dear. My ... child ... My ...

'She missed me. She said that.'

'Yes.'

My dear, dear child.

'But she still can't . . .'

'It's up to you.'

'No. She shouldn't have . . . What did she say in the car?'

'Nothing. We were both quite silent. I dropped her at the gate and she said thank you Jeremy. That was all.'

'I'll talk to her mother tomorrow.'

'You have to have a point of view, you know.'

'She is my daughter.'

He came to me and put his arms around me. He leant his face into my hair.

'I am your lover,' he whispered.

'I don't remember.'

'But now. You must know now. You must have a point of view about that too. You must at least recognise my love, even if you don't feel anything yourself.'

I sighed. I touched his cheek with a finger. I stroked the smooth bone beneath his eye.

'Things happen so fast, well not exactly happen, but present themselves so fast. I feel like some sort of prehistoric snail.'

Jeremy laughed.

'I think I'll go and get the supper,' he said.

* * *

Stephanie and Ciara were just finishing their supper. Ciara was in a bright pink pair of pyjamas and a matching dressing gown, furry slippers keeping her feet warm. Her mother had taken one look at her when she had come in the front door and had packed her off to the bath. 'And wash your hair,' she had commanded as Ciara had gone up the stairs.

'Blah,' said Ciara to herself. 'Blah, blah.'

She had lain for a long time in the bath thinking about her father; then she had thought about pain and joy.

Were you able to feel pain and joy at the same time?

How did you know that it was pain and joy that you were feeling?

Pain hurt, she knew that; hurt like little knife wounds, little stabs in vital places, heart, head, soul.

Where anyway was your soul situated, she wondered, except in your head?

Joy, on the other hand, lifted you up above the ground. You felt a wonderful lightness of being as if you were levitating, stress- and pressure-free above the ground.

Unsustainable.

Yes.

That was the one bad thing about joy; you always knew in the back of your mind that it was unsustainable.

Pain, on the other hand, might be with you forever, for all your life.

Drudgery.

Yes. That was it.

Perhaps I shouldn't have asked him such a thing.

Perhaps I was just drunk on the wonderful novelty of him being again in my life; it had made me dizzy in the head.

I am still dizzy in the head when I think about him, like a lover, I suppose, but with lovers there always has to be anxiety, like with joy the serious possibility that this euphoria will end. I have no such feeling. All I know is that he has to love me. He may go again as he has done before, but always, always he must love me. I am his child.

Unequivocal love.

Yippee.

She submerged herself beneath the warm water and all thoughts ceased; her hair floated and twisted on the surface and, most pleasurably, her ears filled with water.

'Blah,' she said once more to herself. 'Blah, blah, blah.'

✳ ✳ ✳

'You what?'

Stephanie threw her knife and fork down onto her plate and stared across the table at her daughter.

All round Ciara's face her hair had dried into delightful tiny question marks.

'I simply do not understand. Why? Why?'

'He's my father ...'

'Aren't you happy here with me?'

'Yes, of course. I just want—'

'If you're happy here with me, you just stay until you've done your leaving, then you can do what you bloody well like. Bouncing backwards and forwards between Henry and me for the next year and a half is not going to do any good for you.'

'I want to.'

Her mother shrugged.

'That's as may be, but we can't all have everything we want. You can go to him for weekends and holidays, but this is where you should ground yourself. However, I'll talk to him tomorrow.

I'm sure he'll agree with me and of course there's always Jeremy to think of.'

'Why? What has it to do with him?'

'Now you're really being stupid. They're—'

'He must see . . .'

'See what, for heaven's sake?'

'I want to be with my father.'

'Use your reason, child . . .'

'I am not a child.'

'Well you're behaving like one. No one is going to stop you going to see Henry whenever you want to, but you can't just upset everyone's lives like this. He has to get back on his feet again, Jeremy and he have to adjust to living as a couple, and that won't be easy and you just want to hurtle out of my life and into theirs. Just think about what you're trying to do. Think.'

'You're being so unreasonable.'

'I am being unreasonable?'

'Yes.'

'Well just think what you're being.'

She got up from the table and stood looking down at her daughter.

'A pain in the neck.'

She left the room.

'Blah, blah, blah.'

✻ ✻ ✻

'Au clair de la lune . . .'

My mother was singing.
To me?
I don't really know.
Moments of domesticity with Tash were rare.
But she was singing.

'Mon ami Pierrot.'

Her voice wasn't bad at all, sweet and pitched low.
I sat by her knee, happy for the moment.
I clapped my hands together in time to the tune.

'Prête moi ta plume,
Pour écrire un mot.'

It was a summer day, the silence filled with not just her voice, but also the buzzing of flies; and somewhere in the grass a grasshopper ticked. The sun hung above us in a cloudless sky.

'Ma chandelle est morte,
Je n'ai plus de feu . . .'

The sand was warm under my bare feet.
She sat on a small camp stool and sang, her face lifted towards the warm sun.

'Ouvre-moi ta porte,
Pour l'amour de Dieu.'

In front of us, between us and the sea, was the canvas on an easel, on which she had been working until she took it into her head to sing. The sea was breaking on the sand, waves curling as they seemed to reach out towards us. They curled, uncurled in time to the tune of the song. The sand was dusted with fine grey stones and broken shells. A slight wind rippled the water behind the waves.

'Au clair de la lune,
Pierrot répondit,
Je n'ai pas une plume,
Je suis dans mon lit.'

Her voice dropped almost to a whisper and her fingers stroked my hair.

'Va chez la voisine,
Je sais qu'elle y est,
Car dans sa cuisine
On bat le briquet.'

'What does that mean?' I asked her.

She looked shocked, as if she had forgotten that I was there, and suddenly and quite roughly she pushed me away from her side.

'Go,' she said. 'Go and play with George. Now. Leave me in peace. Run along.' And as she spoke she reached for her brushes and was lost to me.

The picture she had been painting that day hung in my sight, just over the fireplace on the other side of my room to my bed; as I lay and looked at it I heard the echo of her singing voice.

'Au clair de la lune,
Pierrot répondit . . .'

Fading away, away, away. The sun was shining outside, reflected in the snow, windows glittered. I must get up, unaided, I thought, and go and see Stephanie.

I manoeuvred my way out of bed. I sang a little song as I made for the bathroom.

'Au clair de la . . .'

I laughed.

Soon, I thought, if I keep this up I will be climbing every mountain, running over the Featherbed, playing Federer at tennis.

There was a knock on the door.

'Henry.'

'Good morning. I'll be out soon. Ready for coffee.'

'It's Stephanie on the telephone.'

'I'll ring her back in ten minutes.'

'She's coming round.'

'I'll call her back. I'm washing my teeth, dammit.'

'She's on her way. Now. This moment.'

Dammit.

I spat. Pink toothpaste and that disgusting slime that coats the inside of your mouth while you sleep swirled in the tap water.

'Can I help you dress?'

'No. I can manage.'

'I'll make some more coffee. Hot.'

I didn't answer.

I heard his shoes shuffle away across the carpet. He stopped. He coughed.

'Henry.'

I stood by the basin and stared at my face in the glass.

God, I thought, I look old and grumpy.

'What?'

'Do you want me to go out for half an hour or so? Leave you in peace with her. Would that be the best thing?'

I opened the door and looked at him. He looked as if he hadn't slept well.

'I want you to stay here, be with us and speak. Whatever happens you are an integral part of it, so stop being so bloody feeble-minded about the whole thing.'

I held out my arms towards him and he ran into them and we stood there, two unkempt middle-aged men, quite still for a few minutes, our hearts thudding together. After a while I pushed him gently away.

'Hot coffee would be great, and necessary.'

*   *   *

They sat, the three of them, in the sitting room; Jeremy staring out of the window at the snow still falling from the green-grey sky. The other two were side by side on the sofa, facing him, and their coffee steamed gently on the table in front of them. Stephanie had swept in half an hour earlier, thrown off her coat, kissed Henry, waved at Jeremy and settled herself on the sofa.

'Well,' was the first word she had said. She looked from one man to the other.

'Have some coffee?' suggested Jeremy.

'A little milk and two spoons of sugar. There are times you need sugar and there are times you don't.' She looked like she had stepped straight out of the bath into her clothes and had left the house without attending to her hair or face. 'Now I need it.'

'Calm down,' said Henry, sitting beside her. 'Old pet.'

She looked outraged.

'Don't you old pet me.'

'Hey, hey. Don't attack me. The child sprang it on me too. I had nothing to do with it. Absolutely nothing. I promise you that. Had I, Jeremy?'

Jeremy shook his head morosely. He fiddled with the coffee pot, but didn't take his eyes from the window.

'Does she hate me? What have I done to her? Oh God! I always tried to be a good mother. Honestly. After you left, I did try so fucking hard and look at both of them now, she wants to go, get out, and Donough's ...' She looked from one man to the other. 'Well, you know. I don't mind. I've told him I don't mind, but honestly, deep inside myself I do. Is that my fault too? What have I done wrong? How can I ... how can I? And now she wants to leave me. I don't know. I didn't sleep a wink. I kept trying to work out ... what the hell ...'

Tears burst from her eyes. Henry pulled a handkerchief from his pocket and shoved it into her hand. She covered her face with it.

After a while, Henry touched her arm.

'Look, old umm ...'

'I didn't mean to come and bawl all over you.'

'That's OK. Bawl away. She loves you. She's only a child and I think she feels she's been given an enormous present. I'm back in her life and she wants to make sure I'll never get away again. It's a bit sick and a lot childish but she'll come to terms with whatever we decide. As for Donough,' he shrugged, 'that has nothing whatever to do with you. You've always been wonderful, calm, fair, loving, right up in the top one per cent of great parents.'

'She wants to go.'

'No, she doesn't. She's confused. She's sixteen. She hasn't thought about it properly. What I think is, let the hare sit.'

She removed the handkerchief from her face and stared at him.

'What the hell does that mean?'

'Just let her calm down. Tell her we'll talk about it all after Christmas. Tell her we both love her and we don't want to hurt her in any way. Waffle at her, if she wants to know. She may just have decided to leave things alone for the time being. Send her round to me. I'll say the same as you.'

'How do I know?'

'Stephanie! Come on.'

'I'm sorry. I didn't really mean that. I just feel wrecked and my brain has stopped working.' She took a drink from her cup. 'Nice coffee. Great coffee. Why does my coffee never taste as good as this?'

'We get our beans blended,' said Jeremy.

'Would you get me some for Christmas, just like this?'

He laughed.

'No problem.'

'You're a nice man. I really do hope that you'll both be very happy together.'

'Thank you.'

Henry took her hand in his and kissed it.

Her eyes filled once more with tears.

'We mustn't get sentimental.' Gently she pulled her hand away. She blew her nose with a noisy flourish and they all laughed again.

'Why do we laugh?' she asked to the air.

'We have to. It's this country. If we didn't laugh we might drown in our own tears.'

'Such rubbish you talk, Henry.'

Jeremy got up and walked over to the window.

'Take away this cursed gift of laughter and give us tears instead.' He intoned the words as he watched the dancing snow.

'Who said that?'

'Someone who did not want to subscribe to Henry's notion of the country sinking beneath the weight of tears. Personally I prefer laughter, from the mild giggle to the uproarious burst. Very therapeutic. Such fools we mortals be.'

'Motley's the only wear,' whispered Henry.

Jeremy clapped his hands together.

'There, you see, even Shakespeare agrees.' He bowed towards Stephanie.

'Any more coffee? I think you're both nuts.'

'No. We're trying to find out about ourselves. We don't want to make any more doleful mistakes, this is why Ciara's demand is somewhat inopportune. The coffee's finished.'

'I'll make some more.' Jeremy picked up the coffee pot.

Stephanie got to her feet.

'No. Don't bother. I must go home and get dressed. I must pull myself together. I've done nothing yet for Christmas.

There's so little time. Would you two collect George from the airport? That would be so kind, and drop him off with me. Keep him safe from Tash. He'd like it so much if you would do that.' She wrapped her head in a large silk shawl. 'He'd like the feeling that we all want him here.'

'Tell me something.' Henry stood up slowly and stood holding on to the back of the sofa. 'Do you love him?'

'We all love George.'

'I don't mean that.'

'I know what you mean and you know as well as I do that I don't. You were the brother that I loved, foolishly enough. I might have been better off with George. He's a decent man and we all love him and I'm so pleased that he's coming home for Christmas and maybe we will be able to persuade him to come home for ever. Maybe. Then we might all live happily ever after.' She turned to Jeremy. 'You met George at your sister's funeral. Remember?'

'He seemed a nice guy.'

'Very.'

'What can we do, or bring, apart from the coffee?'

'Just yourselves. I must fly. Goodbye.'

She was across the room and out of the door before they could collect themselves.

*   *   *

The next morning the snow stopped. The gutters ran with water; snow slithered from the burdened branches of the trees onto the pavements below. Drips fell from window ledges, roof gutters, eaves and of course the trees. The world had become khaki-coloured; even the sea crawled uneasily, burdened by long white rollers, green and brown and grey, touching the land and the rocks and inlets from Scotsman's Bay round to Killiney with distaste. No blue, no sun and a raw east wind which cut through people's clothes, their hall doors and even through the thick walls of mansions in Killiney. Nobody was safe from that wind. It made people think disagreeable thoughts.

Stephanie turned up the central heating. Then she settled herself at the kitchen table with a large cup of coffee and made lists; present lists, kitchen lists, George lists, to do lists, not to do lists. When she had drained her coffee mug, she picked up all the pieces of paper and tore them up.

'So much for lists,' she said. She threw the shreds in the dustbin.

The telephone rang; it was Tash. Her voice was blurred.

'Why is George not staying with me?'

'Darling, we've discussed this . . .'

'I'm a lonely old lady. He's my son. He ought to stay with me. I'm alone.'

'Tash, we've made all—'

'Don't argue with me Stephanie. He is my son. He's not your son. He's not even your brother-in-law any longer. He's not your . . . anything.'

She stopped talking and Stephanie could hear her having a quick drink.

'We'll talk about it tomorrow,' she said hopefully.

'Now,' said Tash. 'I'm coming round.'

'No. It's horrible out. Tomorrow. Come and have lunch tomorrow.'

'I have ordered Mr Cook. He will be here in ten minutes.'

'Oh well ...'

'So I will be with you in twenty minutes.'

'Lovely, darling. Look forward—'

Tash put down the receiver.

Twenty minutes almost to the dot, Mr Cook's car splashed its way up the drive. Stephanie had the hall door open in a flash and watched as Mr Cook got slowly out from the driver's seat and opened the back door for Tash. He leant into the car and unwrapped his passenger from a red and green rug and held out his hand to support her out. It was a struggle, but she made it, clutching her handbag to her side.

'Wait, Cook, I won't be long.' She touched Stephanie on the shoulder and tottered into the hall, where she began to unwrap herself.

'Your house is too hot. Bad for you, very bad for the furniture, no air to breathe. I hope you have coffee ready. I always give people warning so that they can have coffee ready. Not that I go many places these days. No. I definitely do not. There's so little time left, why waste it, I say to myself, on people. People can be so boring. The kitchen I presume.'

Stephanie followed her into the kitchen, where she settled herself in the big wicker chair near the Aga. She began to rummage in the bag.

'Don't fill the cup to the top, dear, I have to put in a few medicinal drops.'

With a flourish she produced half a bottle of whiskey from her bag.

'Medicinal,' she repeated, as she poured. She took a drink,

sighed and settled herself back among the cushions.

'Will I bring some coffee to Mr Cook?' asked Stephanie.

'Good God no. He probably hates the stuff. He'll be quite all right. He has a radio in his car these days. Now, tell me why did you want to see me?'

Stephanie sat down at the table and stared at her mother-in-law; the old lady looked quite demented, she thought, her head and her hands shook and her eyes were bright fires.

'I . . . ah . . . just thought it would be nice to see you. It's been ages. Are you all right? It's been so horrible. I . . .'

'No. No, I'm not all right. But you're not to tell the boys. I can't work. It is weeks now since I was able to work. My hand shakes and I can't seem to put the paint where it needs to go on the canvas. I am not well at all.'

'Have you been to the doctor.'

'Doctor!' Her voice was filled with contempt. 'What use is a doctor? How can a doctor tell me where to put the paint on the canvas?'

'He might be able to stop your hands shaking.'

'He might fill me full of poison. He might put me in the hospital. I want to die, as die I must, unhelped by doctors. How old am I?'

Stephanie shook her head.

'I think I am earmarked for death.'

'Don't be silly, Tash. Don't even think such a thing.'

'I dream. Such dark dreams. What was the name of that woman Henry married? You know, the one you let him go off with?'

'Tash . . .'

'She inhabits my dreams.' She poured some more whiskey

into her coffee. 'I don't believe in heaven or hell, nothing like that. I think that dying is a door into peace. She can't be right when she beckons me. I can't sleep in case she comes too close. If she touched me I might never wake again. She has no peace; I do not want to leave the world under her auspices. No. I can tell you that. Charlotte, that was her name.'

'Yes.'

'You should have married George.'

'I didn't love George.'

'Well, you should have. I have always known that Henry was gay. Always, always. Even before that awful woman rang and told me what he had been up to with her son. I told him he should tell you, not lead you on and on with his blinking charm. He always wanted to be better than George. Win. He always wanted to win. Here, take this.' She held out her cup of coffee. Stephanie took it and put it on the table. Tash held out her shaking hands towards her.

'Look,' she screamed. 'How can you paint with hands like that.' Not only were her arms shaking, but her hands were gnarled with arthritis, her fingers like little stumps of branches, brown and withered. 'How can I work? How can I live, if I don't work? Call Mr Cook. I must go home. He must wrap me up and I must go home.'

'Why don't you stay here, Tash.' She captured a shaking hand as she spoke and it squirmed and trembled in hers like some tiny frightened animal. 'Stay here. Come upstairs to bed and sleep a while and then we can think. Stay here till after Christmas. Please. Let me mind you.'

'No,' shrieked the old woman. 'I want to go home. Cook.

Cook, come and save me. I must go home. I must paint. I have so little time left.'

She tore her hand from Stephanie's grip and struggled to stand up. There was a knock on the back door and Mr Cook's voice calling.

'It's right, madam, I'm here.'

Stephanie opened the door. He was standing there with the red and green rug over his arm.

'I heard her calling,' he said. 'I thought she might. I was listening out for her. She hasn't been well recently.' He walked across the kitchen and wrapped her in the rug. 'There, madam, everything will be all right. I've come to bring you home.'

The sound of his voice calmed her. She leant her head wearily against his shoulder.

'Cook,' she said. 'It is time for me to go home. How splendid that you should arrive.' She smiled at Stephanie. 'Cook always arrives.'

'Yes. That's great. Mr Cook, I think she should stay here.'

He picked the old lady up in his arms.

'Madam would rather go home. I will see her in and make her a cup of coffee. That would be the best thing.'

'Yes,' said Tash. 'That would be the best.'

She shut her eyes and he carried her across the kitchen, out into the hall. Stephanie scurried beside him, picking up Tash's discarded clothes as she went. She opened the hall door and the wind swept in startling them for a moment. He opened the back door of the car and gently manoeuvred her in. He piled her clothes and scarves beside her, shut the door quietly and turned to Stephanie.

'She'll be all right. She was at the bottle all night I think. Mrs Cook'll pop over this evening with a bite of food for her. We know her ways.' He stepped into the car and was off, the old lady sleeping in the back seat.

What in the name of God am I to do about her, Stephanie wondered as she closed the door. She went back into the kitchen and poured herself some more coffee.

I only wish I knew her ways.

* * *

She rang Henry.

His voice was morose.

'It's nothing to do with Ciara. It's Tash. She came round this morning; well to be exact, she's just left.'

'Tash?'

'Yes.'

'What's the matter with her? I haven't seen her for an age. She seemed all right then, maddish but all right. Is she ill?'

'She's really ill, Henry. She's going demented and she's drinking like a fish.'

'So what's new?'

'Don't be flippant. She was in a terrible state this morning. She's like a shadow of herself. I don't think she's eating. You must, you must go and see her. Something has to be done.'

'The doctor . . .'

'She won't go near the doctor. You know that perfectly well. She's frantic because she can't paint. You and George will have to do something.'

'Like what.'

'I don't know. A nursing home, hospital, somewhere she'll be looked after.'

'She'll die if we put her in a home.'

'She'll die if you don't. You should have seen her.'

'Tttttt.'

'Mr and Mrs Cook are being wonderful. You should talk to them. You've got to do something, Henry.'

'Perhaps George . . .'

'You have to do something. At least go and see her. I have no idea whether she'll let you in or not, but you must try.'

'Tttttt. All right. I'll get Jeremy to drive me round. You wouldn't like to come too?'

'No, I would not. I'd leave it till this afternoon, if I were you. She was out for the count when she left here.'

'Old pet . . .'

'Enough of that.'

'Old pet,' his voice was firm as he spoke the words, 'thanks for letting me know. I'll deal with it. I really will. Don't you worry any more.'

'Just make sure you do.'

She put down the receiver.

She had to make mince pies; she had taken the day off from work to make mince pies, so she would go and do it, knead, flour, roll and fill. Concentrate, forget mad or perhaps merely drunk Tash; forget Ciara, just knead, flour, roll and fill. She switched on the radio, fortissimo, and began to bake.

* * *

'As soon as Christmas is over we will go away. Tell me somewhere you really want to go.'

They were stopped at traffic lights just beyond Blackrock on their way to Tash's house in Merrion Avenue.

'Thailand, Oz, Inja, Japan, California.' He paused as he shifted gear and turned left into Merrion Avenue. 'Turkey, Morocco, South Africa.'

Henry held up his hand.

'Stop! I'm much more modest. Expensive and modest at the same time. I'd like to go to Venice and live like a lord: the Danieli, Harry's Bar, water taxis, I couldn't yet manage all those bridges and steps, so water taxis everywhere, a few short strolls to look at the shops, evening concerts, exhibitions in the daytime and a few long rests each day, watching the Venetians sauntering by. Next best thing to Paradise.' He sighed. 'In my dreams.'

'No dreams. We'll do it. Or perhaps there's someone you would rather go with.'

Henry turned towards him and put his hand lightly on Jeremy's thigh.

'No. In the whole world, no. You are the person, dear friend. Next turn on the left.'

Some of the houses had Christmas trees in their gardens, charming and gaudy in the darkness of the afternoon. The third one along was Tash's. There were no lights of any sort to be seen. Jeremy stopped outside the gate and they considered the darkness in silence.

'I have a key,' said Henry, rummaging in his pocket. 'You know we can't realistically make any plans . . . until . . .'

'I know.'

The wrought iron gate was standing open and they went in and along the flagstone path and up the steps. He rang the bell, which jangled in the distance. There were no signs of anyone moving, no lights came on. He took the key from his pocket, but before putting it in the lock he rang the bell once more.

'Yoo-hoo, Tash,' he called as the door opened. The air was tired, cold and lonely; behind him Jeremy closed the door and switched on the light. It was one of those charming Irish houses with its principal rooms on the top floor and then the rest downstairs; bedrooms and living rooms were jumbled together, some upstairs and some down. There were five open doors round the hall, a sitting room, a study, two bedrooms and a bathroom. There was no one in any of them; each room was neat and clean and cold. Henry leant over the top of the stairs.

'Tash. It's Henry. Tash.'

They went down the stairs.

Through the glass in the back door was a glint of light.

'She's out in the studio.' He was so relieved. He opened the back door and switched on the yard light. 'You stay here. I'll just go and see if she's OK.'

'Mind those cobbles, they're very slimy-looking.'

'I'll be all right. I'll take great care.'

He slowly set off across the yard.

'Hey, Tash.'

A shadow moved behind the glass in the door. The sound of a key being turned.

'Who's there?'

'Henry.'

'Well get the hell out of here. How did you get in?'

'Tash, it's Henry.'

He tried to open the door, but she had locked it. She banged on the inside of the door.

'Get away. There's nothing here for you to take. I have my telephone here and I'm going to ring the police. And my son. I'll ring my son.'

She began to mutter to herself; Henry was just able to hear the rhythm of her voice.

'Tash, listen. This is Henry.'

'Go to hell.'

'Henry. I am your son.'

'My son is in Canada. Toronto. I am going out to live with him.'

'I am not George. I am Henry.'

She laughed.

'No, no, no.'

'Open the door and you'll see.'

'No, no. You're not Henry. Henry's in hospital. He may be dying.'

'I am Henry.'

'Go away. I tell you. You don't sound like Henry.'

'I assure you—'

'I am going to call the police.'

Her shadow moved away from the door.

'Tash. Tash, come and look out of the window. You'll see who it is.'

'Go away.'

A light came on in the kitchen of the house next door.

'What's going on out there?' a woman's voice called. 'Are you all right, Tash?'

'This is Henry here. Is that you, Mavis? She won't let me in.'

'Hello, Henry. I'm glad you're better and out and about. You've come to see your mother?'

'She won't let me in.'

'Oh dear. She's gone a bit odd, you know. Will I come round and see what I can do?'

'That would be very kind. Jeremy will open the front door for you.'

'I'll just be a tick.'

Henry stuck his hands in his pockets and jiggled up and down to keep warm; water splashed in the drain that ran across the yard and dripped from the roof and the surrounding trees. There was silence from the studio. He wondered what she was up to. Softly she began to sing.

'I'm a rambuler I'm a gambuler, I'm a long way from home, and if you don't like me,' her voice got louder, 'well leave me alone. I'll eat when I'm hungry, I'll drink when I'm dry and if the moonshine don't kill me, I'll live till I die.'

She began to laugh. A raucous, scratchy laugh.

Henry sighed. This should not be happening.

She started to sing again.

'I'm a rambuler, I'm a gambuler, I'm . . .'

Mavis, wrapped well in a fur coat, appeared beside him. Jeremy stayed just inside the kitchen door.

'Hello, Henry. How good to see you looking almost well again.' She made a swooping kiss on his cheek. 'Now, what's all this?'

He made a helpless gesture with his hand.

'. . . a long way from hoooome.'

Mavis knocked on the door.

'Tash.'

'Hooome.'

'It's Mavis, dear. Open the door and let me in?'

'I can't.'

'Whyever not. Please, Tash, be good and open the door. It's very cold out here.'

'My hand won't turn the key. My hands have stopped working. Did I tell you that?'

'Let me in and I'll have a look at them. A little massage will do them the world of good.'

'A massage?'

'Yes. You remember that nice woman did your back once. We could go to her tomorrow. But you have to let me in first. Just turn the key slowly. You can manage it if you try.'

'Slowly?'

'Slowly.'

'What was her name?'

'Whose name?'

'The woman who used to sing that song.'

'Which song?'

'I'm rambuler, I'm a . . .'

'Oh God, what the hell was her—'

'Delia Murphy,' Henry whispered at her.

'Yes. Yes, of course. Delia Murphy.'

The door opened slowly and Tash peered around it at them. She looked past Mavis, directly at Henry. She pulled the door open wide and opened her arms towards him.

'Henry. Darling boy. You've come to visit. Come in, come in. You too Mavis, and whoever that is lurking over there. We'll have a little party.'

He felt himself held in her warm embrace, warm and memorable; his head was filled with memories and love. Her arms shook as she held him to her. She kissed his neck and his hair and as she kissed him she pulled him into the studio, warm and smelling of turpentine and rotting oil paint just as he had always remembered it. Memory flooded and flooded and with her incoherent but loving words the mists were swept away in the flood.

'I'll put the kettle on.' As she spoke Mavis threw her fur coat over the back of a chair.

Tash let go of Henry.

'No. Wine. We must have wine. Henry, your friend must open some wine.'

'Jeremy. Have you met my mother? Tash, Jeremy.'

Jeremy crossed the room and kissed her hand.

'Charming. There's some quite decent St Estèphe on the table. Would you?'

'I must go, darling. I should be getting the dinner.'

'Nonsense, Mavis. Just a glass. A celebratory glass. My son is well again and visiting me. We must celebrate. Glasses, Henry darling. Before you all decide you must go away. Before I am alone again.'

Henry took her by the arm and put her sitting on a chair.

'Will you have something to eat, Tash?'

She shook her head.

'Only Mrs Cook,' she said. 'She gives me food. Just Mrs Cook. Other people try to poison me.'

'Don't be silly, dear heart. Nobody wants to poison you.'

'You'd be surprised. Stephanie tried earlier in the day. Mr Cook rescued me. Like St George, just in the nick of time.'

'Who wants wine?' Jeremy held up the bottle.

'You see, I can't manage to open wine bottles any longer, because of my arms, so I only drink whiskey.'

'Where do you keep the glasses?'

'Now, I wonder, where do I keep the glasses? You know, Henry.'

'I'll find them.'

'Anyway I don't mean Stephanie. I mean that other person you were married to. The one that caused all the trouble. Did you know that there'd been trouble?' she asked Mavis.

'Well . . . er.'

'Yes. We all knew about that. Anyway I think she was the one.'

'Oh do shut up, Tash.' He was wandering round the studio looking for glasses. He gathered a few dirty ones up and took them over to the sink. It was filled with plates and cups. 'You're not being sensible. You're dreaming all this rubbish.'

'Henry never spoke to me like that. You're not my Henry. Who are you? Are you a doctor? I told that woman I didn't want a doctor.'

'Have a glass of wine.' Jeremy put one into her shaking hand. 'That's Henry all right, it really is. His nerves are bad since his accident, so don't have a go at him. Just love him like you did when you saw him first.'

She turned to Henry and threw her arms around him again.

'Poor Henry, dear Henry. No one loves you like your mother. Will you come with me to live in Toronto?' She turned to Mavis. 'I've always wanted to live in Toronto. My son George has invited me out to live with him. You know George, don't you?'

'Of course I know George. He's a lovely chap. You'll be very happy out there with him.'

'Just the three of us. I will mind my two boys, just like I used to. It will be wonderful and all those nice Canadians.'

Everyone laughed and held their glasses up.

'To nice Canadians.'

Tash laid her head back on the cushions.

'I'm tired. You may all go now. I shall sleep a while and Mrs Cook will bring me some food.'

She looked again at Mavis.

'Do you know Mrs Cook?'

'Indeed I do, and Mr Cook.'

'Good. That's good.'

Jeremy just saved her glass as it fell from her hand.

She was asleep.

The three of them looked at each other.

'What do we do now?'

Mavis picked up her coat.

'Well I, for one, am going home to get the dinner. Mrs Cook will be coming round, you know. She comes every evening. She brings her food and tucks her up for the night. He sits outside in the car and reads the paper. He's there if she needs him. I'd creep out if I were you. She won't wake now till Mrs Cook comes. There's nothing you can do. I have a key. Sometimes

Derry or I pop in before we go to bed, just to see if she's all right. She is very distressed, you know, about not being able to paint. She won't have the doctor in the place ... that's just a warning in case you think of bringing him round. Well, I must be off.'

'Good night, Mavis, and many thanks for your help.'

'No problem. She's a sweet old girl. We just try to keep an eye on her.' At the door she stopped. 'You wouldn't be thinking of putting her into a home, would you?'

'I haven't really thought ...'

'Because I think that would kill her. So if you want to kill her do that. Otherwise, I think we can all manage with things as they are. It can't be for too long. Poor old Tash.'

She went out, closing the door behind her. The two men watched her cross the yard stepping carefully on the slimy stones.

'Sweet Jesus Christ. What do we do now?'

Jeremy didn't answer him. He wandered round the studio, picking up empty tubes of paint, dirty brushes, hard with paint and age, and scrapers. There was a board with mixed colours, a couple of broken knives and an easel with a canvas on it covered with desperate blue and orange streaks of paint that meant nothing. Ashtrays overflowed and the top of the table was covered with burns. A large sketchbook lay open on the table with deep scribbles like an angry child might do covering page after page. There was a ladder up to a gallery which ran round three of the walls; canvases were piled willy-nilly up there, leaning against the walls or jumbled into heaps on the floor, gathering dust. Dirty cloths mouldered everywhere, hanging from the gallery, on the table, heaped by the sink or scattered over the floor. He heard a moan and turned; Henry was standing near his mother's chair with a small rug in his hand, tears rolling down his cheeks. Jeremy ran and put his arms around him.

'I just wanted to cover her with this and I couldn't. I just began to ... oh sweet Jesus how can this have happened to her? Is it my fault?'

Jeremy took the rug from him and gently placed it over the old lady's shoulders.

'There. That'll keep her warm. Of course it's not your fault. It's time, age, bloody age, it does it to so many of us. Not your fault, old pet, not your fault.'

'What'll we do?'

'What will we do?' He rubbed at the tears on Henry's face with a finger. He bent and kissed his cheek. 'We'll go home. She'll be all right. Mrs Cook is coming. The amazing Mrs Cook. Somehow we'll all hold on until after Christmas. Don't worry. We'll find someone to come and look after her. We won't put her in a home. After Christmas. After Christmas, old pet.'

Henry threw his arms around Jeremy's neck and the two men kissed. The old lady slept with a tight little smile on her face.

✳   ✳   ✳

The next morning I woke with the comfort of his arms around me. He was browner than I had ever been and the soft fair hairs that covered his arms shone like gold in the sunlight coming through the window. I hardly dared to breathe in case I might wake him and he would move away. His breath was warm on my neck, it smelt of yesterday's smoked cigarettes and wine, that didn't bother me. His leg moved beside mine and I heard myself give a little moan.

'Finished?' he asked.

'Finished what?'

'I've been watching you watching me for an age.'

'Two minutes.'

'Much much longer. You like what you see?'

I ran a finger up his arm through the golden hairs.

'I like. I really do.'

He laughed, a huge triumphant laugh.

He crushed me to him; he hurt my tender ribs, but I didn't care. For that moment I didn't care.

'There's something I must say. Something I meant to say last night but—'

'You chose to get smashed instead. You drank and bellowed and cried and passed out. I had to sling you into bed.'

'And then.'

'Sling myself in beside you. So speak. Say what you have to say. Then we must get up and face whatever the day will throw at us.'

'Will we be frivolous forever?'

'If that's what you want, old pet.'

'Yes. I think it is. The searching in my head has really exhausted me and now it seems to be over. I did tell you last night, didn't I? I think I shouted it at you. It was the shock of that house. Tash. It's all come together, flooded me. I was, yes, flooded . . . except . . .' I lost the words.

'Except what?'

'Her. I cannot remember her. Nothing about her at all. Her hair, her smell, her voice. Did she really exist?'

'Charlotte? Of course she existed. This was her flat. It was in her car you had the accident. She was bloody driving. Of course she existed. That's just a blip in your brain. My sister. I'll get you pictures of her.'

He moved. I clutched at him.

'No, no, no. I believe you. I'm just saying that she has been wiped out of my mind. I remember this flat. I know where my shirts are and the corkscrew, stuff like that, but I do not remember her. Nothing about her. You tell me she was beautiful — gone. You tell me she owned this flat — gone. You tell me she loved me — gone. All bloody gone. There is a hole in my mind as far as she is concerned. I can see this bedroom, but never her. I can see the sitting room. I remember the evening you came back from Australia, but I cannot see her. I had never seen you before and there you were, like magic, the one person I wanted in my life. I do remember that. That extraordinary feeling. YES! I shouted inside myself. This is what it has all been for. This man. This turmoil inside me ever since I was a child, ever since I could remember. You walked through the door and I knew. You smiled at me and I knew. You took my hand and I knew. You made polite talk and I knew. But she is not in that picture, never before, never since. And now our life begins. Yes?'

Jeremy nodded.

'After Christmas,' he said.

✻ ✻ ✻

217

Three tins of mince pies, two plum puddings, neatly wrapped in their bowls, thirty-six meringues, one slab of pâté de campagne, two sides of smoked salmon, one joint of spiced beef, wrapped in butter muslin, and a ham, glazed and cooling on the shelf in the pantry. Christmas is almost here.

Stephanie took off her shoes and put her feet up on the sofa in the sitting room.

'We won't starve,' she said aloud to the empty room. 'I may of course die of exhaustion.' To stave off such an eventuality she took a long deep slug from the whiskey glass that stood by her on a table.

For two days she hadn't given a thought to either her daughter or her mother-in-law; Ciara had kept out of her way, or rather, Steph thought sourly, the way of the beating, chopping, stirring and grinding that had been going on.

As for Tash?

The Tash problem could wait till Christmas was over; when everyone was lying around gorged and hungover, then they could start to think about Tash. Poor old Tash, but one thing, she is not coming here to live. Oh no.

On Boxing Day they would sit around, those involved people, and sort out the whole thing. I wonder would Mr and Mrs Cook move into her house. We'd have to pay them a hell of a lot, but it couldn't be for very long. Could it? She thought about all the people she had known who had lingered on for years trampling on the love that people had had for them, turning it into bitterness and tears; wringing withers. That made her smile; what is a wither, she wondered. She took another drink.

She could not be taken away from her house, that was for

sure, or her paraphernalia, her brushes, tubes, boards and canvases; and her memorabilia, bits and pieces from her long life, who knew when she might want to summon up some tiny fraction of the past. She must be safely warm; safe and warm, yes, that was very important. After Christmas, Boxing Day. Her eyes felt heavy, she wondered where Ciara was and it wasn't as if she hadn't been a good mother. She had another drink. She felt angry with her daughter. I was a good mother. I am a good mother. I look after her and I give her space. I don't probe; other mothers probe, pry, are filled with ridiculous imaginings. I trust her. Yes I do. Bloody hell. She had another drink and then contemplated her empty glass. No, she thought, no more. I'm a bit pissed, I'm tired, I'm fed up. She got up and poured herself another large splash. This is not a good idea. No. She sat down again. She had a picture of Tash in her head. She's not mine, she muttered, then remembered silly things from the past, kind things. Little presents, evenings at the theatre, the odd book that Tash had pressed into her hand. You will adore it, she would whisper. Sometimes she had, sometimes she hadn't, but the thought was memorable, affectionate. Had she, Tash, been a good mother? According to her own view of the mother's role she hadn't been bad, she had primarily been herself, a painter; the boys came after that. Nannies and people had protected her from them, and of course them from her. Just as important. She took another drink. She lay right back into the cushions. Even after Henry had left, Tash had continued with her kindnesses; lots of women wouldn't do that, they remained deeply loyal to their own child and never saw the rejected spouse. Not Tash. Tash always appeared to have some secret that she found amusing about Henry. She had known the way he was, known and never told a soul, had laughed inside herself. She wondered what she would have done had Tash told her all those years ago. Disbelieved her? Let things lie, shrugged her shoulders and said who cares? Married old George? That would always have been a possibility. She giggled. No. Not that. He was the nicest man she knew, but not for marrying. I won't even marry him now, not even when I'm facing into old age. I don't need that.

Her eyes were heavier now. She had trouble in keeping them open. I think I must go to bed. I am facing into old age. Tash will die and we will have a mighty funeral, and Ciara will leave home and I will ... whiskey slopped over the top of the glass onto her wrist.

'Bugger.' She sat up, spilling the liquid everywhere. 'Bugger Ciara. Bugger Tash. Bugger Henry. Bugger Christmas. Bugger old age. Bugger the world.'

Her feet held her — she had been afraid that they wouldn't — and carefully she made her way across the room and the hall and up the stairs to bed.

*　*　*

Dublin Airport was like a lunatic asylum: people going away, people coming home, people meeting people, packages, parcels, suitcases, trolleys, people standing angrily in long queues or bursting out like river floods through dark doorways, wave upon exhausted wave, people, searching with their tired eyes for familiar faces.

'We should have told him to get a taxi,' said Jeremy.

'George wouldn't do that. He's not a taxi person. He'd rather walk. He's full of probity and common sense.'

'You make him sound boring.'

'No. Not that. He's immensely kind ... and calm. But definitely not boring. I suppose I drove him out of the country.'

Jeremy laughed.

'Get away!'

'He wanted to marry Steph. I couldn't let him do that.'

'Why on earth not?'

'I thought I would be happy with her and she loved me. And she didn't love him.'

'How do you know?'

'She married me, didn't she? We were happy or something like it for years, until ... you know, you two played your joke on me.'

'The pursuit of happiness is a dangerous thing.'

'But very seductive, my darling. What do you think we are pursuing?'

'This is an odd place to be having a conversation like this.'

There was a sudden surge of people out of the two arrival doors.

'Do you think death will be like this? People bursting into an immense waiting room, anxiously looking for a friendly face. Someone to show them the way.'

Henry laughed.

'For God's sake, what a thought. I just have a picture of empty space and a great wind blowing. There he is, look there. George. Man with the largest suitcase in the world. Hey, George. Here.'

He waved. Suddenly he was excited, like a child. He banged his stick on the ground. He felt he might cry.

George saw him and with difficulty manoeuvred himself and his case in the right direction. The waves flowed around him and somewhere a group of people began to sing.

'Once in royal David's city . . .'

'Oh Georgie boy . . .'

'Stood a lowly cattle shed . . .'

He stopped dead as a whole family passed in front of him, children squealing, trolley just avoiding his feet. Happy Christmas they shouted all at once at the elderly pair who were meeting them.

'Where a mother laid her baby . . .'

'Henry.'

'George.'

'Oh man.'

'In a manger for a bed.'

The two brothers stood face to face and then embraced each other.

'Mary was that mother mild, Jesus Christ that little child.'

Jeremy watched them and smiled.

'This is it, man,' said George. 'The very it.'

They embraced again.

Jeremy took the case from George's hand.

'Come on you pair of goons, follow me. Hold on to Henry, George. He's still very shaky on the legs. A slight swish from a trolley might have him sprawling.'

'Yes. Yes, of course. I see the stick, Henry. Father's stick. I remember that stick well. He used to threaten me with it when I made him angry. Never hit me though. Never never. Just waved it in the air.'

'He came down to earth from heaven . . .'

The sound of the singers was swallowed up by the travellers, the meeters, the seekers and finders, the squeaks and rattles from the trolleys, the thousands of feet, marching, shuffling, stamping and then suddenly they were out in the cold winter day.

'We have snow,' said George, looking round.

'We have an east wind that would carve off your bollocks.'

Jeremy put down the suitcase.

'I'm going to go and get the car. Just you two wait here. I'll be about ten minutes.'

'We'll freeze to death. We'll come with you.'

'You'll never manage the stairs.'

'Of course I will. If the worst comes to the worst, George can haul me.'

They panted up the stairs. They stood for a moment at the first landing just to get their breath.

'How's Tash?'

'Ummm . . .'

Jeremy began to walk away pulling the case after him.

'It's just another floor. You wait inside that door and I'll pick you up on the way down.'

'Leave the case, you idiot,' Henry shouted after him.

Jeremy left the case by the door and disappeared.

'We're very anxious.'

'Stephanie . . .'

'Very anxious. We're going to have a serious discussion. She needs . . . she needs . . . well to be honest I don't know what she needs, but a lot of decisions have to be made.'

'She was all right in September.'

'Things have changed. A lot. Her mind slips in and out of reality, she won't eat and she is drinking like a fish. She seems to be convinced that someone is trying to do her in or else lock her up. I must admit I've only been to see her once since I came out of hospital and that was the night before last and only . . . well only because Steph rang me and said I must. I feel grim about this. But now . . .'

'Now what?'

'You must see her.'

'Are you trying to foist her onto me?'

'Don't be an ass. You must see her and then once Christmas is over we must . . . Old pet, it's bad.'

George touched his brother on the shoulder.

'Oh, man,' he said.

A couple of plastic bags blew past them, through the door and along the passage, performed a pas de deux for a few moments and then sank to the ground in a corner. The two men watched them.

'We'll do the right thing. We all love her. Money . . .'

'It's nothing to do with money. That is not the problem, George. It's what is best. What she will tolerate? How can we protect her without her dying?'

'She'll die anyway, for God's sake. She's old. Everyone dies.'

'I don't want to cause her death. I want to keep her safe. I want her to be happy – no, no what a stupid thing to say. I want her to not be frightened. That's better. That's more like. Yes.' He stared bleakly at his brother's suitcase, wishing that his mind would work with clarity, wishing that his power over words would be supreme, wishing that he could forget everything again. No, not that. Not ever that. I must never wish for that deprivation of my past, of my pattern. Our patterns are important.

He became aware that George was talking to him.

'Sorry,' he said. 'Really sorry, old pet.'

'It's OK. I thought we were going to have a charming family reunion, lovely food, lots of presents, kisses and hugs, all that sort of thing, but in reality we're having a crisis.'

'We're putting off the crisis till Boxing Day. Stephanie has worked like a slave to make Christmas just like you said. We've all got to— here's Jeremy. Do you mind if I go in front? There's more leg room.'

The car drew up beside them and George put his case in the boot and then got into the back.

'If it's all right with you,' he said, 'I'd like a bath and a sleep before anything else happens. Can you drop me at Stephanie's house?'

*   *   *

Stephanie was pulling back the curtains in the sitting room when the car turned in at the gate; she always loved pulling back those curtains, letting in the first light of the day. They were the colour of crushed strawberries, rich velvet with cream silk linings, and she had had them made the summer just before Henry had left. She always pulled them slowly caressing the velvet with her fingers and tied each one back with a deep red silk rope. The room was full of flowers, ready for visitors.

'Ciara! They're here.'

There was a scuffling in the hall and Ciara in her dressing

gown flew out of the hall door. She opened the back door of the car and pulled her uncle out.

'You see we have snow. Especially for you.' She gestured round the garden, then threw her arms around him and hugged him.

'You call this snow? My God, child, you haven't lived. You couldn't prance around in your bare feet where I've just come from. Go in. Go in, foolish girl. Stephanie, call your undressed daughter in out of the cold.'

'Welcome George. Happy Christmas. Are you two coming in? Cup of tea? Coffee? Breakfast?'

Henry rolled down the window.

'No. We won't. Thanks. He should go to bed quickly. For a couple of hours. We'll call round about two and take him to Tash.'

'I'll do that,' said Stephanie.

'I . . .'

'I'll do it, Henry. It's all right. I want to see her. You can collect her tomorrow. That would be a real help.'

She turned away and bundled the waving George and his case and Ciara into the hall and closed the door.

'Thank God, they didn't come in. You must be exhausted.'

George rubbed his face with his hand.

'I sure am.'

She put an arm around him and pushed him gently towards the kitchen.

'A little breakfast and then bed. We won't talk about anything serious now. What are you doing with that case, Ciara?'

'I'm bringing it up for Uncle George.'

'It's much too heavy . . .'

'Yes Ciara. Leave it. I'll bring it up myself. Coffee is what I long for. A large cup of coffee. No food, darling Steph, just coffee and then a bath and if you don't hear me look in after twenty minutes because I'll have fallen asleep. I might drown. I wouldn't want to drown.' He took her hand and kissed it. He waved towards Ciara who was hovering in the doorway. 'Go back to bed, lovely girl. I'll see you later. We will all be saner later.' He fell into a chair. 'God, how I hate flying, airports, people, dare I say Christmas? A spot of milk please. Do you know this is the first Christmas for years and years that I've spent with anyone. I usually shut myself up and read books. I say happy Christmas on the telephone to my family and friends and then slump. It's great.' He laughed for a moment. 'Luckily I live in Toronto, not Montreal, there I'd have to say it in French.'

'Why don't you bring your coffee up to the bath with you. I'll carry the cup and you can manhandle your case.'

'Steph.'

'Yes. What?'

'Oh, nothing. Just a passing thought. Yes. I'll go up. You're a lovely woman. Know that? Yes. A really lovely woman.'

He grabbed the handle of his case and began the climb up the stairs. Stephanie said nothing, she just followed him, carrying his steaming cup of coffee.

A couple of hours later he came down again; he still looked tired but he had clean, uncrumpled clothes on and he had a spark in his eye.

He found her in the sitting room carefully cutting paper,

wrapping and tying; around her on the floor were piles of cheerful parcels.

'I don't know what time it is, but here I am. Alive and well.'

She folded the paper and put it on the table.

'Dear George, you do look more human. Come and have some soup and then we'll go and see Tash.'

He followed her into the kitchen.

'Henry told me that she's not well.'

He sat down

'That's putting it mildly. It's most distressing to see her. We really do seem to have neglected her most terribly. I thought we were doing what she wanted. We've been so used to being summoned when she wanted to see us, that it never occurred to me that we were in fact doing what was easiest for us. This is good.' She put a bowl of soup down in front of him. 'There's French bread, or would you rather have toast?'

'Lovely. Lovely. This is perfect.'

He reached out for some bread.

'She may be fine when we go round, but I doubt it, and then you'll think we're mad. She won't see the doctor. Maybe you'll be able to persuade her.'

'I've never been able to persuade her to do anything. Don't you remember?'

'It's different now. You and Henry are the strong ones now.'

'I wouldn't have called either of us strong. Not when it comes to Tash. This soup is gorgeous.'

'I'll bring some to Tash. That would be a good idea.'

She got a plastic bowl from a cupboard and ladled soup into it.

She didn't know what to talk to George about; until the Tash problem was dealt with, chit chat seemed remorselessly idle. She snapped a top onto the bowl, poured herself some coffee and sat down opposite her brother-in-law.

His mouth was rimmed with rich brown bean soup. She pushed a napkin across the table towards him. 'And what's more, bloody Ciara wants to go and live with Henry.'

He laughed. He wiped the soup from his mouth and laughed again.

'It's no laughing matter,' she said severely.

'No is an easy word to say. If you both say no she'll get the message quick enough. Tell her you'll send her to boarding school if she doesn't behave.'

'Such croooelty!'

'Well deserved. Come on. Let's go and see the old girl. Let's really cheer ourselves up.'

The clouds were thick again overhead and from time to time a splash of rain fell onto the soaked earth.

'It's loathsome,' said George as they splashed along the sea front. 'You'd better come and live in Toronto with me.'

'Such rubbish you talk.'

'But you like it. God, but this place has changed, flats, offices, almost skyscrapers. And whatever happened to that cinema?'

'It's progress, darling. You have it in Toronto too, I'm sure. P.R.O.G.R.E.S.S. It's all over the place.'

'I remember that cinema so well. Tash used to take us to see the most unsuitable films. What was it called?'

'The Pavilion. It's a block of flats now, three or four restaurants, several pretty grim shops and a theatre.'

'Oh man!'

Someone had swept the snow from the steps up to Tash's door; they were wet but not slippy. Stephanie rang the bell, then opened the door with the key and called out Tash's name as they went into the hall. There was no reply.

'She doesn't seem to use the house much. She'll be in the studio.'

It was cold. They went down the stairs and out of the back door. Across the yard they could see a light on in the studio.

'Tash,' called out Stephanie.

There was no reply.

No one had swept the yard, and there was a constant dripping from the trees that hung over it. The studio door opened and Tash appeared. She was wearing a dirty dressing gown and had a rug wrapped round her waist.

'Who is calling me?'

'It's Stephanie. I've brought George to see you.'

'Well you can go away. I've got nothing for you. You may not come in.'

She turned to go back into the studio. Steph and George ran to get to the door before she closed it in their faces. George held it open until Stephanie was inside with his mother and then he closed it behind himself. The three of them stood and stared at each other.

'Who are you?' asked Tash, her eyes fixed on George.

'I'm George. I am your son.'

He took a step towards her and she stepped backwards away from him.

'I'm George, dear Tash, your George.'

She laughed.

'I suppose you want something.'

'No. Just to see you.'

'Are you Henry?'

'George.'

'George went away.'

'I'm back. For Christmas. Tomorrow is Christmas, dear.'

'I don't know.'

'I brought some soup. I'll just heat it up. Nice Tuscan bean soup.'

No one paid any attention to her. She moved towards the cooker at the back of the studio.

Mother and son continued to stare at each other.

'I should get my hair done if it's Christmas tomorrow.'

'Steph can organise that, can't you Steph?'

'What's that?'

Was there a bloody clean saucepan in this bloody place.

'Mother would like to have her hair done before Christmas.'

'Oh, sure.'

She picked up the least dirty and turned on the tap.

'What are you doing over there?' The old woman's voice was sharp.

'Heating up some soup for you.'

'I don't want your soup. Mrs Whatsername brings me food. Mrs . . . Mrs. Safe food.'

'Mother . . .'

'I am not your mother. Where is Mrs . . . Mrs Thing. She comes in here. I know her. She comes in here. Mrs . . .'

She wailed suddenly and huge tears splashed down her cheeks. George ran to her and put his arms around her. He stroked her raggedy hair; her body shook against his. She beat at him with her fists.

Steph stood, dirty saucepan in her hand, and watched them both. Old age, she thought, is so hateful.

After a while she calmed down and stood within his arms, her head still on his shoulder.

'There, there,' he murmured. 'There, there.'

She looked up at him and her eyes suddenly sparked with recognition.

'George,' she said. 'George. How wonderful to see you. I was going to telephone you. I was going to come and stay. Wasn't I, Stephanie?'

'Indeed you were.' Stephanie put down the pan, with relief. 'Look Tash, why don't you get dressed and come home with us and I can fix your hair for you? Tomorrow is Christmas Day and it would be nice if your hair was done. We're all going to have Christmas dinner in my house tomorrow, Henry and the kids and Jeremy. George. The whole lot. We're going to have a feast. You must look your best as the head of the family.'

'The head of the family. Yes. That's good. If you will excuse me for a while I will go and get dressed. My clothes are over in the house. We will have to go over there. It may be rather cold.'

'I'll turn on the heating.'

Tash took George's arm and the three of them marched across the yard, Tash's rug trailing in the mud.

'Do you know how to turn on the heating?' Tash asked as they went in the back door. 'Will it be safe?'

'Perfectly safe and the whole house will be warm.'

'George will come with me and help me dress.'

It took about an hour to get her organised; the heat was rising in the house and outside snow flakes were twisting down from the grey clouds.

'Will you bring your night things, Tash?' Stephanie asked her. 'And spend the night with us. We'd love you to do that.'

'Certainly not. I can never sleep unless I'm in my own bed. I will come home when you've done my hair. Mrs Cook will be popping round with my supper.'

'I could telephone her and—'

'Certainly not.'

'She might like the evening off.'

'I am her first care. She will be coming round with my supper. I have to give her her orders.'

'Tash . . .'

'Let's get going. I am not going to argue with you, Stephanie. We'll do it my way or I won't come at all. I will have to get Mrs Cook to do my hair.'

'All right, all right. You win.'

'They understand me.' She put out a hand and touched George's cheek tenderly. 'Not even you, my love, understand me like they do. So, let's go. I presume you have some drink in your house?'

'More than even you would need, my dear.'

The rest of the afternoon was spent in frantic activity: the remaining parcels were wrapped, the table laid, glasses on the sideboard, potatoes peeled, celery washed and cut, bloody Brussels sprouts cut.

'Why do we have to have Brussels sprouts?' Ciara asked

George.

'Someone must like them.'

'Not me.'

'Nor me. Let's not do them then. Let's throw them in the dustbin.'

'No, no, George. It would be as much as your life is worth. Stephanie cannot imagine Christmas dinner without the little buggers.'

Stephanie led Tash to the bathroom, turned on the bath and filled the water with aromatic smells and oils.

'Give a shout when you're out and I will come and do your hair. Do you want me to help you undress?'

'Certainly not.'

As Stephanie closed the bathroom door, she heard the clink of bottle and glass. She sighed and went downstairs.

'Oh lovely,' she said as she went into the kitchen, 'you've done the sprouts. I'm always tempted not to do them, but someone would be bound to complain. What is the name of Donough's boyfriend?'

'Brendan.'

'Brendan. Yes. I must not forget, my head is in turmoil. He might complain. He might say: No Brussels sprouts. I can't have Christmas dinner without them and get up and leave.'

The three of them laughed.

'I think a glass of wine would be good. How about you, Steph?' said George.

'I dare not. I must not before I do her hair. It's got so thin and depressed-looking, I might cry as I chopped.'

'You mustn't chop, Mum. Very delicate snipping is what's needed.'

'I'll snip, but I must be sober.'

After the washing and the snipping had been successfully done Stephanie had installed Tash in an armchair in the sitting room.

'I used to be very beautiful you know,' she said, moving her head from side to side, feeling the soft curls bob against her neck.

'You still are, darling.'

'Your father used to say . . .' She stopped suddenly and frowned. 'Where is he? He should be here. Isn't this a celebration of some sort? Your father should be here.'

'Grandfather's—' began Ciara. Stephanie started to cough; she went red in the face and clutched at her throat.

'Darling . . . a . . . honk honk . . . glass of water . . .'

Ciara ran out of the room. The coughing stopped.

'There is no need for that sort of carry-on.' Tash's voice was cold. 'I know where he is. Henry has locked him up. It's what he's going to do with me.'

'Tash, don't be silly. Of course Henry hasn't done any such thing.'

'I beg your pardon. I know what I'm talking about. Don't think you can soft soap me. Thank you, I'd love another glass of wine.' She held her glass out towards George. He moved towards her and put his arms around her.

'Darling Mother, he's dead. He died a long time ago.'

She pushed him away.

'Don't, don't, don't say such a thing. I know your father is not dead. You wouldn't know. You are never here. Yes. I am . . . no, no, I must say we are, when your father comes from wherever Henry has incarcerated him ... we are coming to stay with you. Over there.' Ciara came back in with some water for Stephanie. She handed the glass to her mother, who put it on the table.

Tash stood up.

'I must be going.'

'Stay and have supper. I'll drive you home when we've eaten.'

'Mr Cook is waiting. I don't like to keep him waiting for too long.'

'He can't be waiting.'

'I assure you he is.' She got up and walked slowly over to the window and pulled back the curtain. Sure enough Mr Cook was outside, sitting in his car, waiting patiently. Tash waved at him. He got out of the car and moved towards the hall door. Tash smiled triumphantly at Stephanie.

'And Mrs Cook will have food for me when I get home.' She moved towards the hall.

Ciara opened the door and Mr Cook was standing there, with a rug over his arm.

'Cook. What about tomorrow. There is a festival of some sort.'

'Don't worry Mr Cook about tomorrow. Henry says he will pick you up, about one o'clock.'

'Cook will bring me round here. Won't you, Cook?'

'Certainly, madam.'

She took his arm and with great care he led her down the steps to the car.

'Not Henry. I would not be safe with Henry. I am safe with Cook.' She got into the back and he tucked the rug around her.

'By the way,' she said, 'I have no presents for anyone. None whatsoever.'

He shut the door. They all waved. They watched the car go down the drive and turn out of the gate.

'What are we going to do?' asked Stephanie.

'I'm going to ring Henry,' said George.

When he did, there was no reply.

* * *

Christmas Eve.

I woke for the second time.

He stood beside the bed. He was tall and beautiful in the midday light.

Also anxious.

I didn't want him to be anxious. I held up my arms towards him, as a child would do.

He sighed.

He leant towards me. He held me.

Warm and safe.

We didn't speak.

We knew.

That was our Christmas Eve.

I was awakened by his movement; he was sitting up. Outside the window the street lights were sparking in the darkness.

'Don't go.'

'It's the fucking telephone.'

'Leave it.' He slid down beneath the bedclothes again. He began to laugh and I laughed with him. We held on to each other and yelled with laughter.

'I'm starving.' He spoke the words finally.

'Mmmm, now I think about it, so am I.'

'Were there things we should have done today?'

'Only what we did do.'

'Things we told other people we would do?'

'What does it matter?'

'Should we have worried about Tash?'

'Nah. Not today.'

'George?'

'Nah.'

'Do you love me?'

'What do you think?'

'Would you say it?'

'I love you. Now you.'

'Yes. I love you. Forever.'

'Sssh.' I put my finger on his lips. 'Never say that. It is only a word. A dangerous word. You may think it, but don't say it. Please.'

'I take it back. I will never say forever again.'

'Old pet.'

He got out of bed.

'I'm going to have a shower and then make us some food.'

The telephone rang again.

'I won't touch it. Not today. It can ring and ring.'

'What time is it, anyway?'

'Six thirty.'

We laughed again, for a day well spent. A Christmas Eve, and we laughed and laughed and oh God, it was such a happy time.

Christmas Day

The sun was shining.

That surprised everybody.

People smiled and shouted across the road to each other.

'Happy Christmas.'

Some wag even shouted 'Top of the fucking morning,' and the people he had shouted at laughed.

It was that sort of day.

The snow that had fallen on Christmas Eve had frozen and crunched under people's feet.

The church bells rang in the frosty air.

Henry and Jeremy slept very late, curled into each other's arms.

Donough and Brendan got sprucely dressed and went to have drinks with friends.

Tash, her soft hair bobbing on the back of her neck, sat in her studio wondering why she had put on her best clothes.

Why?

Where was she going?

She had to be going somewhere, she thought.

But where?

I used to be very beautiful, she muttered to herself.

Yes. I remember that.

Men used to turn in the street and look after me. She looked down at the gnarled, shaking hands.

No use, she thought.

No fucking use.

He used to hate me swearing and now I can't remember his name. If I close my eyes I cannot even see his face.

I'm a rambuler, I'm a gambuler . . .

How can I remember that trivial song and not his name or face?

What is memory?

Just a word.

Where might I be going today?

Where was I yesterday?

Was I anywhere yesterday?

I am so tired and my hands won't stay still.

I was very beautiful.

Oh yes.

I do remember that.

Or do I?

Is it not just words that I remember.

Words.

Did I paint these pictures that surround me?

I don't remember.

Old hands. Do they remember the feel of canvas, of chalk,

charcoal, pencil? Do they remember how to hold a paintbrush, to draw a line with authority across a page or a canvas?

Do I know who I was?

What did I do with my life?

What is life?

Another word.

Why am I sitting here in my best clothes?

Why am I?

✼ ✼ ✼

Stephanie was woken by the bells of two local churches, battering the air with happiness. The door opened and Ciara came in; she came over to her mother's bed and put a cup of tea on the table beside Stephanie's head.

'Happy Christmas.'

'Darling. Thank you. How lovely. Perfectly lovely.' She pushed herself up among the pillows. 'Happy Christmas to you too.'

They made kissing noises towards each other.

'I just wanted to say I'm sorry, about the other day.'

Stephanie reached out and took her daughter's hand.

'I must have just been a little crazy. I don't want to go and live with Henry. I'm quite, quite happy here. I love you.'

'Sit down, darling.' Stephanie shifted her knees to make room.

'I don't know why it came over me, but it's gone now. I want to stay here with you. I want to see lots of Dad. I like Jeremy, I really do, but I think he'll probably hate me for a while after what I did the other day.'

'Of course he won't. I must say Tash had pushed the whole thing out of my mind. I'm much more worried about her than I was about you. I just felt aggrieved about you. I thought you were being bold and provocative.'

They kissed, cheek to cheek.

'May I open my presents now?'

'Certainly not.'

'Please.'

'You're being bold and provocative again. We're all going to open our presents before dinner, when everyone is here. Now, I must get up and put the turkey in the oven. You can make the breakfast and bring George a cup of tea.'

'I have. He just snored at me.'

'Well, we'll leave him to snore then. He's jet-lagged and shocked.'

'Just one present?'

'No presents. Scoot away and leave me to prise myself out of bed.'

By one o'clock everyone was there except Tash, the first glasses of champagne had been drunk, the food was sizzling and bubbling, the gaily wrapped presents were piled around the tree watched over by a slightly sulky Ciara.

'In five minutes I am going to start opening my presents,' she said.

No one paid any attention to her.

Donough was sitting at the piano.

'Somewhere over the rainbow ...'

'Cut it out, Donough.'

'Skies are blue.'

Henry joined in the singing.

'Tra la lalala ...'

Brendan sighed.

'Anything need doing in the kitchen?'

Stephanie laughed.

'Believe it or not, all is ready. You'll just have to put up with the singing.'

'Like Ciara, I want my presents. I want everyone to have their presents. The best thing about Christmas is watching other people opening their parcels.'

'Shock, horror.'

'There's that certainly, but also there's good stuff.'

'If happy little bluebirds ...'

'No. No, no. That's the end. Look, Donough, start again. Come on, Ciara, over here, George, you know the words. Brendan ...'

'Count him out, Dad, he hates community singing. Give the lad more champagne. Mum? You with us?'

A chord.

'OK? Let's take it away.'

> 'Somewhere over the rainbow,
> Way up high,
> There's a land that I dreamed of,
> Once in a lullaby.'

No one heard the bell except Stephanie and she slipped out of the room humming the tune as she crossed the hall.

'Somewhere over the rainbow, skies are blue,
and the dreams that you dare to dream
really do come true.'

She opened the door.

Mr Cook was there with Tash clinging to his arm.

'Happy Christmas,' they all said simultaneously.

'I'm sorry we're late. Madam was a little confused. But she's all right now. Aren't you, madam?'

Tash didn't say a word. Her face looked dark.

'Won't you come in, Mr Cook, and have a glass of champagne?'

'If happy little bluebirds fly beyond the rainbow . . .'

Tash's face lightened.

'Happy little bluebirds,' she said. She smiled at Mr Cook. 'Excuse me a moment.' She let go of his arm, and gathered her long bronze cashmere shawl around her shoulders; she brushed past Stephanie as if she had never seen her before.

'Somewhere,' she sang as she crossed the hall. She opened the sitting room door. 'Over the rainbow, skies.' The singing stopped for a moment and there was a cheer and the door shut.

Mr Cook watched her progress with a certain anxiety.

'She said she didn't want to come, but she seems all right now. I hope you won't have any trouble.'

'Don't you worry, Mr Cook. She'll be fine. We'll look after her well.'

He bowed slightly.

'I will call back for her this evening.'

'There's no need . . .'

'I would prefer.' He bowed again and went back down the steps towards the car. He turned and waved; she waved back.

'Happy Christmas,' she muttered to herself as she closed the door.

She stood for a moment in the hall; Christmas was all around her, holly, ivy, mistletoe hanging from the lamp above her head; candles flickered on the mantelpiece, deep bronze chrysanthemums were on the table, the smell of food and the sounds of laughter. She heard Mr Cook driving off, a chord on the piano, a moment's silence and then Tash's voice.

'Somewhere over the . . .' The others backing her. 'Rainbow, way up high.' La la la la. 'There's a land that I dreamed of . . .'

Stephanie smiled to herself. It was going to be all right. Christmas would pass, decisions would be made, life would go on, there would be sadnesses and joy and people would die and be born . . . Oh shut up she said to herself, let's get on with opening the presents.

She opened the door and went in; Tash was standing with her back to the tree. Her hair was brushed upwards and highly lacquered, giving the effect of a silver halo. She spread her arms wide, the bronze shawl fluttering like wings as she moved her arms.

'Once in a lullaby.'

She looked Stephanie straight in the eyes and threw her head back.

'If happy little bluebirds fly beyond the rainbow, why, oh why . . .'

She was the diva. They all stood and watched her with awe, waiting for the high note.

'. . . can't . . .'

She stopped and looked round, keeping them in suspense. For a split second she looked puzzled.

'I?'

She fell backwards, sending the stacked parcels flying. She hit the tree, which swayed for a moment and then fell and she fell with it and the tree and the parcels and Tash became a multicoloured heap on the floor. The tiny candles flickered and then went out and baubles crunched and everyone looked in silence.

'Mother. Tash. Help, someone help. We must get her onto the sofa.'

He put his arm around her shoulders and lifted her head.

'Her eyes are open.'

Stephanie was there beside him.

'What'll we do? Steph. Her eyes are open.'

'Let's get her onto the sofa. Here Donough, Bernard, lift her up. Gently.' As the two young men lifted Tash up, she took Henry's hand. 'Darling, I think she's . . .'

'Her eyes are open.'

'And air. Give her air. Put her there on the sofa and open the window. Ciara, run and get a blanket, there's a good girl. George, some water, please.'

Everyone sprang into activity.

'Oh, my God. Oh, my God,' someone was muttering.

Who, wondered Stephanie. She chafed Tash's hand. She stroked her face, touched her neck, tried to feel pulses.

Tash seemed to be shrinking in front of her eyes.

'Steph,' Henry whispered in her ear. 'Steph, Steph.'

'Shut up,' she said. 'Bloody well shut up.'

He sobbed.

'Is she going to be all right?'

'No.'

He sobbed again.

'Well ... how do I know ...' George shoved a glass of water into her hand and she began to drink it.

'No.' She wet her finger and ran it over Tash's lips. There was no reaction. Ciara arrived with a blanket. 'Thanks love. Give your father a drink. Sit him down somewhere. Keep him sitting down. We don't want ...' She tucked the blanket round the old lady and George put a cushion behind her head.

'She's gone? Isn't she?'

Stephanie nodded.

'I think so.'

'Poor old Tash.' He stroked her hair gently. 'Poor, poor old lady.'

'Will I make coffee, Mum? Jeremy is holding on to Dad.'

'Good girl. That would be great – and turn off all ovens, pots, pans while you're in there. Get Donough to give you a hand. I'll come out in a few minutes. We have to think what we should do.'

'What a way to go.' George put his hand over her face and when he removed it her eyes were closed. 'I've seen that done on the movies and I never knew whether it would work or not.'

Stephanie stood up and looked around at the others.

'Would one of you call an ambulance?'

'No,' said Henry. 'I won't. The doctor. Her eyes are open. She—'

'Her eyes are closed now, Henry. You may come and see.'

'Brendan. Please. There's a phone in the kitchen and another one in the hall. You can tell them she's—'

'No,' said Henry. Jeremy helped him to his feet and they came over to the sofa.

Brendan nodded and left the room.

Henry looked down at his mother for a long time. He touched her hand, he touched her face, his hand fluttered over her hair.

'Did we kill her?' He looked at George.

George smiled at him.

'She just died, bro. In the nick of time. If you believed in God you could say that he rescued her, but if, like me, you don't, she just dropped off the tree. Wasn't she lucky.'

He put out a hand and grasped his brother's shoulder and tears jumped from his eyes. 'We can cry,' he said. 'We can cry for what we remember and for what may be in front of us. All that. Or we don't have to. I will. I will cry, brother. For what she taught me and what she should have taught me. For her jokes and her rages, for her painting. Sometimes I loved her and sometimes I hated her and there were times I never gave her a thought. I will cry for me and you and all the rest of us. Idiots that we are. A whole world of idiots. I will cry because I never came home to see her until now and I never invited her out to Canada. A whole world of idiots. I will cry today and tomorrow and for the rest of my life when I think of her. Poor old Tash.'

Someone clapped. It was Ciara by the door.

'Bravo, Uncle George.' With grace she crossed the room and put her arms around his neck and kissed his wet cheek. 'Bravo.' She handed him a table napkin. 'You might need this,' and everyone laughed for a moment.

'It's coming. It will be about twenty minutes.'

'Thank you, Brendan.'

Stephanie looked round the room again.

The fallen tree and broken baubles ... we could clear that now. No. Wait until the ambulance men had come and taken her away. She wondered if she should give them money, decided no. They could open their presents, that would be untimely. Perhaps they should be put away till another time. She thought of Ciara's face and said no to herself again.

Tomorrow. And tomorrow.

The fucking dinner, she thought. All that work and stress. We'll eat it cold tomorrow and we'll open our untimely presents tomorrow. That's when we would have decided on Tash's future. Instead, we'll eat our cold dinner; and cry perhaps.

'I think we'll all have a drink while we wait. That's the one thing I am certain she would have liked us to do.'

There was a murmur of agreement.

Brendan circulated with the bottle topping up their glasses.

They stood in a semicircle round the sofa.

Henry held his glass up.

'Tash.' He said the word in a crumbling voice.

'Tash.'

He had in his head the grinding sound of metal and the engine's squeal as if it were being pushed beyond endurance and then a voice crying Noooo, which was probably his voice, pitched so hectically that even his mother wouldn't have recognised it.

'To all of us poor foolish mortals.'

They drank the toast in silence.

K